A Match for the Amish Teacher

AMY GROCHOWSKI

Trust in the Lord with all thine heart; and lean not unto thine own understanding.

In all thy ways acknowledge him, and he shall direct thy paths.

Proverbs 3:5-6 KJV

C hapter One

     Michael Beller sat in a darkened far corner of Lydia's Amish Shoppe. Debating.

An email invitation to his brother's upcoming June wedding flashed at him from the small screen on the computer used only for business. Only sending this email to Anna Roth wasn't exactly business. He drummed his fingers on the desk in front of him. Still debating.

If he got up the nerve to hit send, what would she think? What did he want her to think?

He wasn't sure of anything, only that he'd wanted to meet her for several months now. They'd corresponded frequently over the translation of a nineteenth-century journal, which had been donated to her grandfather's Mennonite Museum. The tedious language work would be easier in

1

person, for sure, but he hadn't had an opportunity to travel all the way from Prince Edward Island to her hometown in Ontario to do so.

His forefinger hovered over the right-click button on the mouse. Even alone in the shoppe, his conscience brought up all the opinions he was likely to hear once he pressed that button.

Inviting Anna to his brother's wedding was a thinly veiled excuse to finish the journal translation. But that wasn't all there was to it. Nay, it was an excuse for something else altogether—to stop the matchmaking schemes of his students' mothers, which were ballooning out of control since he'd been announced as the new teacher for their Amish school.

These women would be the Amish PTA—if there were such a thing. In his mind, he thought of them that way. If Anna showed up for the wedding, maybe they'd conclude he was already courting someone. Then she'd go home to Ontario, and he'd go on about his business—minus the persistent hints about one's niece or the other's cousin.

How did they think he was supposed to focus on being a *goot* teacher for their children if he was constantly sidelined by their suggestions for courtship? They ought to be thankful their first male Amish schoolteacher was single-minded.

Not that he never planned to marry. Just not now. Starting as New Hope's newest schoolteacher at the end of the summer was enough of a challenge for him right now.

Still, he couldn't send an invitation to Anna. Michael released the mouse and rubbed his hand against his thigh.

Even though Michael only knew Anna through her letters, she seemed like a nice woman. Asking her to come to a wedding to get the matchmaking hounds off his trail was a big ask. And he wasn't so naïve about women that he didn't understand his request would offend most of them. For sure, he didn't want to offend Anna.

They were colleagues, but also friends. He looked forward to her letters and enjoyed the translation work, and she'd openly written that she shared that pleasure.

It wasn't worth jeopardizing all of that just to catch a break from whatever matchmaking plots the Amish PTA had conceived for this wedding.

The jingle of the bell above the store's entrance made him jump. He couldn't see around the partition separating the computer desk from the rest of the shop but guessed Lydia had returned to lock up her shoppe for the evening.

Of course, it could be Joel, Lydia's husband, and their local minister. With a reflexive tap, he flicked the monitor off.

As he stepped around the partition, it wasn't either Lydia or Joel but their daughter with her back to him, switching the open sign to closed.

"Oh, Samy, it's you. I was just leaving." His heart rate eased.

Not that he'd been doing anything wrong, but being discovered by his soon to be eighth grade student was better than explaining his actions to her father.

Samy whirled around, and her hand flew over her heart as she gasped.

"Sorry. I didn't mean to sneak up on you." Michael tried to look serious, though it was difficult. Her prayer *kapp* was helter-skelter to match her windblown red hair, most likely from riding her horse. Samy never just rode. She galloped across the fields of every Amish farm in New Hope.

"I didn't know anyone was here. *Mamm* sent me to lockup." She stood there with her hands on her hips, presumably expecting him to leave.

"I'm sure she thought I was finished using her computer by now." Michael said, but he wasn't done. And he certainly didn't want to leave that email open. "Do you think she'd mind if I take a few more minutes?"

Samy's eyes narrowed. "*Mamm* said to close the shop and not to dilly-dally. It's almost time for supper." Samy, always exact in following directions, edged around him and aimed for the computer.

Michael backed in front of her and stretched an arm against the partition wall.

She ducked under his elbow.

Before he could stop her, she clicked the screen back on.

He squeezed his eyes shut, then opened them to an image of wild poppies. He let out a breath of gratitude for the screensaver. His message to Anna was covered safely.

Until a click on the keyboard flashed his email back onto the monitor.

"Samy." He tried to reach around her, but she hunched over the keyboard, blocking him as she scanned the page. "It's rude to read other people's mail."

"What?" She glanced back at him. And he almost believed the innocent look on her face.

How she'd known he was hiding something was a mystery he didn't have time to solve.

He lunged for the keyboard to shut down the tab, but the window didn't close. Instead, his misdirected click had sent the email.

Samy placed a hand over her open mouth and glanced back at him with widened eyes.

The blood flow to his legs must have stopped because suddenly his knees buckled. Maybe his heart had stopped, too. He grasped the chair and plopped down onto the seat.

He closed his eyes again and attempted to calm himself with a long breath.

"Do you think she'll come?" Samy's voice echoed his own thoughts.

Michael inhaled again and prayed for patience. When he looked back at her, Samy had moved away to lean against the partition wall with her arms crossed.

"Dear Anna." Samy pointed at the screen. "You asked her to come to the wedding. Do you think she will?"

Nay, he didn't think Anna would come. The moment that message was sent, he knew he'd made a mistake, but there was no way he was explaining his predicament to a fourteen-year-old. Besides, she already knew way too much.

"I agree. She shouldn't." Samy's matter-of-fact tone made him bristle.

Despite having a few reasons of his own for agreeing with her, Michael still asked, "And why not?"

"Because I heard Ada say that her niece was coming to meet you. And Sarah has already invited one of our cousins, who needs a husband. And—"

"Samy, I get the picture." All of which led to his invitation to Anna in the first place. "But as you read…" He inhaled deeply to calm his temper at that invasion of privacy. "I didn't invite Anna as part of a courtship."

"That's why she shouldn't come. You asked her to pretend. That's a terrible idea."

"Well, Samy, I hadn't actually sent it, had I?"

"It's not my fault. I didn't write it."

Nay, this was all his own fault. And now, his most reckless idea ever was soaring through cyberspace to Anna's inbox at her grandfather's museum.

"Are all those women really that desperate?" Samy wondered out loud.

"Thanks, Samy. Do you always rub salt in other people's wounds?"

She either didn't understand the figure of speech or simply ignored it.

"Well, what I think is that they'll be coming for the excitement of a trip to the island and all the wedding stuff that all the girls talk about. But

I'd be embarrassed to go somewhere just to try to get a man to marry me. Don't you think it's embarrassing?"

"I'm really that bad, am I?"

She looked him up and down, then shrugged. "You're the same as anyone else."

"No one is just the same as anyone else, Samy. You know that. We all have equal value in the sight of *Gott*, but He created each of us unique." Still, the truth was that women had never been overly interested in him. And Samy was probably right. They'd come for the fun of a wedding, maybe even hoping to meet a suitor. Only Michael wouldn't be the one to catch their attention.

"I just know I wouldn't want to come if I was Anna—not from an invitation like that. But—" Samy tapped a finger at the computer screen. "If Anna thinks you're special, then maybe she'll come."

"Unless she only shows up to see the island and have fun at a wedding, right?" He'd kind of hoped Anna might at least come for that reason, if not for him.

"Well, then, she'll just be like the rest of them, I reckon, so why bother? Unless she's special to you. But you already told her she's not." Samy stepped around the partition, then called back to him. "I really have to hurry. *Mamm* doesn't like me to be late for supper. Can you shut down the computer?"

"Of course." Michael quickly re-read the email he'd accidentally sent.

Samy was right. Anna shouldn't come in response to such a selfish request.

He was an idiot.

Michael logged off the email and shut the computer down, then went out the front door so Samy could lock it.

"Samy." He called after her as she skipped down the steps and headed toward the Yoders farmhouse. "You really shouldn't read other people's mail."

"I was turning off the computer to close up the shoppe, like *Mamm* told me to do." She responded over her shoulder and kept going.

Michael was going to have his hands full when school began. Probably spending a lot of time on his knees in prayer, too, mostly about this eighth grader in particular.

Between Samy and the three of his younger brothers still in school, Michael couldn't afford to be distracted by courtship and romance. Those four students alone weren't likely to give him an inch of grace as their new teacher. Who knew what challenges the rest of the class would bring?

Still, the last thing he'd wanted was to end the translation work with Anna.

Deciphering bits and pieces of those journals kept life interesting. The translation work satisfied his love for languages and history, but it wasn't a proper job.

Sure, he appreciated the family dairy farm, but he could milk the cows in his sleep. That's why he'd finally agreed to be the new schoolteacher. He didn't want to leave the Amish, like his brother had done, to find fulfillment. But he needed to find his own purpose outside of farming.

A male schoolteacher was unusual among the Amish, but Michael was used to being different. He'd missed school since graduating six years ago and enjoyed learning. Teaching seemed the logical place for him to be useful to his community with his God-given abilities.

Somehow, he'd imagined Anna would understand the stipulations in his email were only practical. He hadn't meant to insult her, as Samy pointed out in her straightforward manner. He'd only meant to be honest by telling Anna the invitation wasn't romantic. But as usual, he was better at deciphering old, forgotten languages than communicating very well in his own.

He'd likely never hear from Anna again.

Instead, he'd go to his brother's wedding and watch as all the eligible young women invited by the Amish PTA paired off with someone else. For a short second he paused on that realization. Maybe some part of him had actually been motivated to invite Anna as an attempt to avoid the loneliness he inevitably experienced at these kinds of gatherings. With Anna he'd have a friend by his side.

But he brushed the thoughts aside. At least he had the new school term in a few months to look forward to.

Anna carefully returned the nineteenth-century journal to the protective case where she and her *dawdi* kept it. The rare treasure had come to them from a family in Manitoba who'd rescued it from an estate sale. While they couldn't read the journal, written in a combination of eastern European languages, they'd recognized its value and importance to the history of Mennonite immigrants to Canada in the late 1800s. Their decision to donate the journal to her grandfather's museum had kept Anna busy working on its translation in her spare time for almost a year.

But she'd needed help. Early on, she discovered the primary language wasn't Russian but Ukrainian, or some mix of the two, along with additional sections in Polish. She'd been way out of her depth and considered giving up when her *dawdi* put a notice in the Mennonite newspaper seeking translators. They had held out little hope that such a person existed, especially someone who'd also want to help them. Thankfully, their one respondent was also a perfect match for the task.

Michael Beller had quickly become as engrossed in the work as she was. The everyday routines of their Mennonite ancestors on a far-off continent and almost two centuries removed were coming back to life before their eyes. Indeed, that reward alone for their labor was exhilarating.

At least it was all very exciting for two history and language buffs. Her friends quickly lost interest whenever she brought up the topic. Except for *Dawdi*, of course. If not for her grandfather, her intense interest in their heritage and languages never would have begun—or had the means to continue.

"Anna—" Her *dawdi's* voice carried from the front room to the small library room where she was working.

"Be right there." She folded and set aside her meticulously hand-copied pages for Michael to translate. She'd have to find a chance to take them to the post office later.

"Your friends are here." *Dawdi* nodded toward the front of the store before Anna could slip behind the counter to where he stood. "Go ahead. I'll take care of things here."

She leaned across the counter and kissed his cheek, which promptly turned red. Public affection always embarrassed him. He wasn't fond of hugs, much less a peck on the cheek, even in private. But Anna knew he secretly loved it. She always said goodbye to him this way and was the only one who could get away with it. She cherished the special bond between them.

He nodded his graying head at her so that his long beard touched his chest. "Go on now. They're waiting."

"Thank you, *Dawdi*." Anna said, without acknowledging the hidden smile behind his command and went to join her friends.

Her long time friend, Lois, turned to greet Anna first. Her dark hair, tanned complexion and chocolate brown eyes glimmered in the sunlight filtering through the shop-front window. Beside her, their friend Mary's honey-colored hair, creamy skin and sparkling blue eyes were equally stunning. Standing with them both, Anna tried to ignore how dull and plain she felt with her barely red hair, boring hazel eyes, and skin splattered with freckles.

In their hearts, which she knew ought to be her focus, they were all equal in friendship—and had been further back than the age at which their memories began. Born on three consecutive days to parents who were also all members of the same church, they'd known and loved each other since before they learned to crawl.

Anna pushed aside the thoughts of comparison that led nowhere goot. Today, they were going out to celebrate their twenty-first birthdays.

"*Ach*, I forgot one thing." Anna's exclamation gained the attention of both friends. She'd been replying to emails earlier and left the computer on. "I need to turn off *Dawdi's* business computer."

They nodded in understanding and trailed behind her into the small office where their business manager worked part-time.

"Caleb isn't here today?" Disappointment laced Mary's not-so-innocent question. Anna did her best not to roll her eyes.

"Is that why you insisted on meeting me here?" Anna teased. And Mary didn't bother to answer as she feigned a sudden interest in a seashell paperweight on the desk.

Anna choked back a laugh as she leaned down to eye level with the computer monitor, resting one hand on the desk and clicking the mouse with the other to wake up the sleeping machine.

"You have to admit," Lois piped in. Her alto voice tinged with amusement. "It's basically a total waste having such a fine-looking unmarried man confined in close quarters with Anna, who's never given a second thought to a man in her life—at least not any living in the present day."

Anna tried not to groan. That would only further her reputation for becoming tongue-tied on the subjects of men and romance. The computer screen blinked on, and her attention snapped to the flash of a new email.

She read the subject line, which made her hand jump to her heart.

"What?" The alto and soprano duet of her friends' voices chorused behind her. And before she could do anything about it, they'd both latched onto the subject line that had her heart pounding.

Will you be my guest at my brother's wedding?

Well, well. That should have her friends thinking twice about her romantic prospects.

Anna straightened to her full height, still an inch shorter than both friends, and set both hands firmly on her hips.

"Dead men don't send emails, now, do they? Or send special invitations to family weddings?" She stared at the two women whose mouths gaped open. "Or am I so clueless about men that I don't know what this means?"

She was milking it for sure. Whatever reason Michael had for inviting her was not—that. Michael had only ever been professional in their exchanges—friendly, but all about their work. But she wasn't about to let this timely deterrent against the teasing go to waste.

Lois whistled low and softly to keep from being heard beyond the small office walls. "Happy twenty-first birthday, indeed."

Once the resulting giggles died down, Anna shut off the computer. She'd read the full email later when she had a private moment.

Mary came between them and took each by the hand. "I reckon this means Caleb is fair game." She looked first at Lois and then at Anna. "I mean, Lois is practically engaged, and now you might be soon, too."

Lois and Mary began their usual giggling as the three walked hand-in-hand toward their favorite coffee and ice-cream parlor for their birthday treat. Anna considered correcting their assumptions about Michael's wedding invitation.

She hadn't even read the email yet, but she was more than certain Michael wasn't jumping into matrimonial ideas. Still, the minor triumph of actually being invited somewhere by an unrelated and unmarried man—well, she'd just let her friends' misconception slide for a bit.

Maybe even, for this one special evening of celebration, she could ride along on a cloud for a little while longer and experience the novelty of thinking twice about a man.

Michael was... different. What if...?

Ach, what a silly fantasy.

Reality forced her back onto the much-preferred solid ground, where life was safely rooted in facts.

Facts didn't change or run off and leave inconvenient children for other people to raise. That's what romance did. And she didn't want it.

C hapter Two

The rhythmic hum of vacuum pumps filled the Beller dairy barn as the milking system operated at full capacity. Michael wiped sleep from his eyes, his mind still foggy in the pre-dawn darkness. Solar-generated electricity powered their large dairy operation. Fluorescent lights illuminated the clean concrete floor of the milking parlor where his brothers moved with practiced efficiency, attaching and detaching milking units in a synchronized routine they'd performed since childhood.

One week. It had been one full week since he'd sent that email to Anna Roth.

Michael sanitized his hands before moving to the next row of cows, checking each Holstein's udder and wiping their teats clean before attaching the milking unit.

"Good girl," he murmured to the first cow before moving to the next.

His hands worked automatically, following the sanitation protocols and equipment checks that required no conscious thought. This left his mind free to wander to more troubling matters—like why Anna hadn't responded to his impulsive invitation.

"The new schoolteacher looks tired this morning," Myles called from across the milking parlor. "Staying up late with lesson plans?"

Michael rolled his eyes. "Just getting my beauty rest for all those adoring scholars."

"The girls, maybe," Martin chimed in, his youthful voice cracking slightly. At sixteen, he was still growing into his adult sound. "But boys like us would have given a male teacher real trouble?"

"No doubt *you* would," Michael replied with a half-smile. "I happen to know some have more sense and want to actually learn."

"Good thing you've had plenty of practice dealing with troublesome brothers, for the not-so-sensible ones," his *datt*, Herschel, added as he monitored the milk flowing through the pipeline into the refrigerated bulk tank.

The barn door creaked open, admitting a gust of cool summer air along with two figures silhouetted against the gradually lightening sky. Joel Yoder and

Bishop Samuel Nafzinger stepped inside, nodding greetings as they shrugged off light jackets.

"*Guten Mariye*," Bishop Nafzinger called. His beard, longer and whiter than Herschel's, caught the lantern light as he reached for a milking stool.

"Bishop. Joel." Michael's brothers straightened their postures slightly at the arrival of the community leaders. Even Myles, usually quick with a joke, fell into a respectful silence.

Michael felt a familiar tightening in his chest. These were the men who had entrusted him with the district's children—a responsibility he still wasn't certain he deserved. Joel moved to assist with sanitizing equipment while the bishop took a position near the control panel where his *datt* stood.

"*Wie geht's?*" His *datt* greeted the two men. "I suppose you're here to meet the family coming by this morning to buy my wagon?"

"That we are. Thought we'd stop in to see if they'd come by here yet. And we were hoping to borrow a couple of your strong young *sohns* to help us show them a welcoming hand, as they surely have a great deal to unload."

"*Ya*, of course." Herschel gave a quick nod in the direction of Michael's younger brothers. "Soon as milking is done, they'll be happy to help. Right boys?"

"*Denki.*" Bishop Nafzinger rubbed his beard. "It will be a *goot* thing to have a new family with youngies growing up among us. No need for Beulah's farmhouse to sit empty now that she has moved in with her daughter, Rachel. Will be *goot* for Noah and Rachel to have dependable neighbors too."

Michael didn't know the Fisher family, who were moving to New Hope from Ontario with their six children, but they were distant relatives of Joel Yoder and had been welcomed to join their community in New Hope.

"And Michael will have a full classroom for sure." Everyone's attention moved to Joel, whose voice carried the measured calm he used from the pulpit. "I was telling Samy, Owen and Paul yesterday how much they'll benefit from having you as their new teacher."

Michael tugged at his suspenders, uncertain how to respond to praise, especially from Samy's father. The girl was intelligent but challenging, often pushing boundaries in ways that tested his patience. Still, there was something endearing about her directness.

"I appreciate your confidence," he finally said. "I hope I can benefit all my students."

"Don't worry. You will continue to learn as well, of that you can be certain. The one who teaches learns the most." Bishop Nafzinger added from across the milking parlor. "We are very pleased to have a young man so dedicated to learning among us. And now to have you teaching our *kinner* is a true blessing."

Joel nodded in agreement. "After seven years with your sister as our teacher, we've seen the value of stability in the schoolhouse."

Michael's hands paused momentarily in their work. Seven years was indeed an unusually long tenure for an Amish teacher. Most young women taught for only a year or two before marriage pulled them away to other duties.

"Mattie was a blessing to our children," the bishop continued. "But when she decided to focus on the maple farm with Winston, we realized we might try something different in choosing a new teacher this time."

"Different meaning me," Michael clarified, unable to keep a note of question from his voice.

"*Ya,*" Joel confirmed. "The school board discussed it thoroughly. A male teacher is not so traditional but offers certain... advantages."

"Your sister's long tenure showed us the value of a long-term teacher. And we are confident you will not be leaving the community or running off to get married and leaving us," the bishop stated bluntly, causing Michael's younger brothers to exchange glances.

"Stronger discipline for the older boys," Joel added.

The implications settled over Michael like a heavy blanket. They expected him to remain a teacher for many years—perhaps indefinitely. The school board had selected him because they believed he would remain focused and dedicated to teaching. Of course, he'd known as much and was on board with the idea. He felt quite certain he'd be happy teaching as a career.

But if they knew about his email to Anna, would they second-guess their choice? Anna was Mennonite, but not part of their district. If he were truly pursuing a relationship with her, things would be complicated by those differences. Joel and the bishop may not be so certain about having chosen him then.

Perhaps it was a *goot* thing that Anna hadn't responded.

His *datt* returned from the cooling room, wiping his hands on a rag. "Belinda is quite excited about all the folks visiting from out of town for Mark's wedding. She's also a protective mother-hen, a tad uneasy about some of the matchmaking going on."

The Bishop and Joel exchanged knowing glances.

"I believe some mothers on the school board had something different in mind when they agreed to a male teacher," Joel said with a subtle humor.

A soft chuckle passed among the men, though Michael found it difficult to join in. The laughter felt like it was at his expense, though he knew that wasn't their intention.

Michael focused intently on his milking, uncertain how to respond. For sure, he wasn't about to admit he'd invited a woman to the wedding specifically to avoid the matchmaking mothers.

"The mothers' group is already planning welcome baskets for you at the schoolhouse," Myles reported. "Mattie says they've never been so enthusiastic about school preparations before."

"I'm grateful for their support," Michael replied carefully, "but I hope they understand my focus must be on teaching."

"Their support comes with daughters and nieces attached, I think," Martin quipped, earning a sharp look from their father.

As they finished the morning milking routine, Michael's thoughts drifted again to Anna's silence.

Perhaps she found his request too inappropriate to acknowledge. Perhaps his message got lost somewhere in the vastness of the internet. Or perhaps she was simply too busy with her own life to worry over his.

A week of silence suggested she wasn't coming. He ought to be relieved, but he'd also have to face the matchmaking mothers on his own. Still a terrifying prospect.

"You'll make a fine teacher, *sohn*," his father said, placing a weathered hand on Michael's shoulder as they cleaned the equipment. "Don't let yourself be pushed toward anything you're not ready for. A man must follow the path *Gott* lays before him in his own time."

Michael nodded, grateful for his father's support but unable to confess his impulsive email. As he logged the morning's milk production in the record book, he calculated again how many days had passed without response. Seven days.

Through the barn door, he could see his mother watching from the kitchen window and knew there would be more questions waiting for him inside. With or without Anna's help, he would need to navigate the community's expectations somehow.

First though, he had a classroom to prepare.

Eavesdropping was wrong. *Ya*, Samy knew that. But did it count if the adult conversation was too loud to ignore and your presence at the sink washing dishes was in full view of all the ladies talking?

She couldn't see how. It wasn't like she could close her ears.

Besides, she hadn't intended to listen closely or anything. In fact, she'd been minding her own thoughts and watching the hummingbirds on her *mamm's* feeder outside the kitchen window. She'd made a game of counting the seconds between each bird's appearance. Twenty-three seconds. Nineteen seconds. Thirty-five seconds. The ritual soothed her as she worked through her morning chores, something she needed to finish before heading to the Detweilers' farm to help with the horses.

Through the window, she could see her younger brothers finishing their morning chores. Thirteen-year-old Owen was expertly stacking firewood by the barn, while eight-year-old Paul collected eggs from the chicken coop, carefully placing each one in his basket. Both were becoming more capable on the farm every day, though Paul still needed reminders to focus on his tasks rather than chasing after the barn cats.

Samy returned her attention to the dishes, calculating how long it would take to finish so she could get to Rachel and Noah Detweiler's farm on time. Amazon would be waiting for her morning grooming, and the therapy horses needed preparation before the day's sessions. Noah always said Samy had a special touch with the more skittish horses—a compliment Samy treasured more than any other.

"Mark's wedding is the perfect opportunity," Ada's voice cut through Samy's thoughts as the women sat around the kitchen table. "Michael will be focused on family celebrations. It's the ideal time to introduce him to suitable young women."

"My niece Leah is very excited to visit," Sarah added. "She's been asking about the new schoolteacher ever since she heard about him."

Samy's hands stilled in the dishwater. They were plotting to match Michael with their relatives again. Didn't they understand he wasn't interested?

"And my cousin's daughter Heather will be coming as well," Ada continued. "She's a hard-working young woman—already manages her own small quilting business. Very organized, just what a schoolteacher needs in a wife."

"Michael is quite focused on preparing for his teaching position." Michael's *mamm*, Belinda, sure sounded an awful lot like her own *mamm* when there was a warning in her voice—gentle but serious. As Samy had come to learn, that tone meant you better listen. "I'm not certain he's considering courtship just now."

"Nonsense." And there was the familiar note of challenge, so like *Aenti* Sarah. And not one Samy could take with her elders. "A young man his age should think of marriage. Twenty-three and still single—it's not natural for an Amish man to wait so long."

"Especially one as handsome and well-situated as your Michael," Ada added. "He just needs a little... encouragement."

Samy bit her lip to keep from speaking out. The thought of Michael being ambushed by matchmaking schemes at his own brother's wedding made her stomach twist uncomfortably.

Besides, she knew her *datt's* thoughts on the matter. He wanted a male teacher to avoid this sort of thing. It seemed her *mamm* was right, though. Matchmaking would occur regardless of whether the teacher was a man or a woman.

A movement outside the window caught her eye. A large semi-truck was making its way up the hill by their house, heading toward the Detweilers over the hill. She'd rarely seen a big rig on their road.

Could it be for the new family moving into the Erb's farmhouse? Rachel and Noah were expecting their new neighbors to arrive this week.

"Did you see that truck?" Samy blurted out, momentarily forgetting the matchmaking conversation. "Is it the strangers moving into Beulah's old farmhouse?"

"The Fisher family, you mean?" Her *mamm* answered, seemingly grateful for the change of subject. "It could be. They're not strangers, though, Samy. Nathan Fisher is a distant cousin of your *datt's* family."

"They have children about your age," Belinda added with a smile.

Samy turned back to the window just in time to see an unfamiliar Amish wagon down at the bottom of the hill, coming along well behind the truck that had already disappeared over the hill. For a moment, Samy felt an unexpected flicker of interest before busying herself with the dishes.

"As I was saying," Ada continued, undeterred, "we should arrange some group activities during the wedding week. Perhaps a game of softball or—"

"Or perhaps we should let the young people get acquainted naturally," Belinda suggested, her voice firmer now. "Michael has a mind of his own about these matters."

Samy couldn't contain herself any longer. She dried her hands and walked over to the table, leaning close to her mother's ear. "Michael doesn't want this," she whispered, just loud enough for her mother to hear. "It's a bad idea."

Her *mamm* looked up with surprise, but before she could respond, Belinda caught Samy's eye with a questioning look.

"Do you know something, Samy?" Belinda asked gently.

Samy froze, realizing her mistake too late.

Ada and Sarah exchanged glances, probably sensing that Samy was about to be reprimanded. "Well," Sarah said, rising from her seat, "we should be going. The day is a-wasting. Best to get to my canning before it gets too hot."

"Indeed," Ada agreed, also standing. "Thank you for the *kaffi*, Lydia."

After the two women departed, an uncomfortable silence fell over the kitchen. Samy stared at her shoes, wishing she had kept quiet.

"Samy," her *mamm's* voice was gentle but firm. "You're not in trouble. But I think you better tell us what do you know about Michael's wishes."

Samy shifted uncomfortably. "I... I might have seen something I wasn't supposed to."

Belinda leaned forward, concern in her eyes. "What did you see, Samy?"

"I didn't mean to," Samy began, the words tumbling out. "I was just turning off the computer at the shop like *Mamm* told me to, and Michael's email was still open, and..."

"And?" Belinda prompted.

"He emailed someone named Anna. A woman he knows through his translation work." Samy glanced between her *mamm* and Belinda. "He invited her to Mark's wedding."

Belinda's eyes widened. "Anna Roth? The Mennonite scholar from Ontario?"

Samy nodded. She'd already said too much, so she refrained from explaining that he had only asked her to come so people would think he was already interested in someone.

Her *mamm* and Belinda exchanged looks that Samy couldn't quite interpret, but guessed they might have assumed precisely what Michael had hoped for.

Ach, she pressed her lips tightly shut, really wanting to tell them the truth of it, for poor Anna's sake, if nothing else.

"Samy," her *mamm* said quietly, "reading other people's messages is wrong."

"I know," Samy admitted. "I apologized. But now Ada and Sarah are planning all these things, and it's not what Michael wants."

Belinda sighed, looking troubled. "Did Anna respond to him?"

"I don't know," Samy answered honestly. "He sent it last week when I was there. I haven't heard anything since." And she couldn't help but hope Anna had been sensible enough to decline. But then, she also couldn't help but hope to meet this Anna.

Belinda's warm hand touched Samy lightly on the shoulder, ever so briefly. "Thank you for telling us, Samy. I think it's best if this stays between just the three of us for now."

"I won't tell anyone else," Samy promised, relieved that Belinda didn't seem angry.

"You should finish your chores now," her *mamm* suggested. "Weren't you planning to help Noah with the horses this morning?"

Samy nodded, grateful for the dismissal. As she headed back to the sink, she heard Belinda speaking quietly to her *mamm*.

"Michael never mentioned this to me. I'm not sure what to think. And if she were to reject his invitation, I'd hate for more folks to know of it."

"I understand, perfectly. We all protect our *kinner* the best we can from such things. We won't say a word of it." Then her *mamm* whispered so low that Samy strained to hear, "I tried to tell Joel and the bishop that you can't avoid matters of the heart, not even with a male teacher."

Samy's jaw ached from keeping her mouth closed for so long. This wasn't a matter of the heart, and it was a mighty struggle not to tell them so. She returned to her dishes to busy herself, working quickly to make up for lost time.

Through the window, she caught a closer glimpse of the wagon before it crested the hill. It must be the Fishers on the way to Beulah Erb's old farmhouse. Several children were sitting in the back, and a girl about her own age was holding what looked like a carrying cage for a small animal, her attention focused on whatever was inside.

Did the new girl like animals too? Would she ever visit Rachel's horse therapy farm? Then, for a moment, she looked up in Samy's direction before the wagon moved out of sight. An unexpected sense of connection pulsed through Samy, as of a premonition of an important change about to happen.

Samy shook her head, trying to refocus on her task. She had enough to think about without worrying about new neighbors.

Yet somewhere beneath the anxiety about disrupted routines and new people, there was a tiny spark of curiosity about both Michael's situation and the new girl with the animal carrier. The feeling was unfamiliar and uncomfortable, but not entirely unwelcome.

Perhaps some new things could make life more interesting. If she could be brave enough to try.

Chapter Three

Anna stared at the computer screen, Michael Beller's email still open in front of her. She'd read it so many times over the past week that she could probably recite it from memory, yet here she was, reading it again as if the words might somehow rearrange themselves into a clearer message.

"Will you be my guest at my brother's wedding?" The question in the subject line was direct—deceptively simple compared to the actual request in his message.

She pushed back from the desk, gently closing the leather-bound journal she'd been translating before the distraction of checking emails had derailed her evening work.

The small office at the back of her grandfather's museum was quiet this time of evening, illuminated only by the amber glow of her desk lamp and the blue-white light of the computer screen. Through the doorway, she could see display cases holding artifacts of Mennonite history—each item carefully preserved, cataloged, and safely contained behind glass. Much like her own life, she thought wryly.

She reached for her notebook where she'd listed all the practical reasons against accepting Michael's invitation:

1. The cost of travel to Prince Edward Island

2. Taking time away from the museum during summer season

3. The ridiculousness of pretending to be someone's companion

4. Unfamiliarity with New Hope's particular Amish customs and community expectations

5. The undesirable task of sewing a new dress for such an occasion

It was a perfectly reasonable list. Her friends might tease her about overthinking things, but Anna preferred to call it a thorough analysis. And her analysis clearly showed that accepting this invitation was impractical at best, foolish at worst.

Yet she hadn't declined.

With a sigh, she turned to a fresh page in her notebook and reluctantly added a second column: "Reasons to Consider."

1. Face-to-face collaboration on the journal translation

2. A scholarly study of the Amish and Mennonite communities from Ontario to PEI

3.

Her pen hovered over the page. There was another reason she couldn't quite bring herself to write—simple curiosity about Michael himself. Their correspondence had been almost entirely academic, focused on deciphering the multilingual texts and discussing historical contexts. Yet occasionally, his letters contained glimpses of something more—a dry sense of humor, thoughtful observations about life on the island, and a depth of character that intrigued her.

"Still working, Anna?"

She startled at her grandfather's voice, quickly closing her notebook. Elmer Roth—*Dawdi* to her—stood in the doorway, his tall frame slightly stooped with age, but his eyes as sharp as ever behind wire-rimmed glasses.

"Just finishing up," she replied, gesturing to the journal. "I thought I might get a few more pages copied to send to Michael before the end of the week."

"Ah, your Ukrainian expert." *Dawdi* nodded, moving into the room with the measured pace of someone who'd spent a lifetime handling fragile artifacts. "How is your collaboration progressing?"

"Well enough. His insights on the Ukrainian passages have been invaluable." She hesitated, then added, "Actually, I received an unusual email from him last week."

"Oh?" Her grandfather settled into the chair across from her desk, his expression curious but patient.

Anna turned the computer screen slightly so he could see the email. "He's invited me to his brother's wedding on Prince Edward Island. As his... guest."

"I see." *Dawdi* leaned forward to read, adjusting his glasses. His expression remained neutral, but Anna detected a slight lift of his eyebrows.

"It's not what it sounds like," she hurried to explain. "He's not inviting me romantically. In fact, he's quite explicit that it's the opposite."

"Indeed." A small smile played at the corners of her grandfather's mouth as he continued reading. "Let me guess. He wants you to pretend to be his companion to discourage matchmaking attempts from the mothers in his community."

"Exactly." Anna's fingers worried at the edge of her notebook, not overly surprised her grandfather would put two-and-two together so quickly. "It's completely inappropriate, isn't it?"

"Is it?" *Dawdi* leaned back in his chair, studying her face. "You've been corresponding with this young man for nearly a year on scholarly matters. Meeting in person seems a natural progression in your working relationship."

"But under false pretenses?" Anna shook her head. "I'd be pretending to be something I'm not."

"Would you?" Her grandfather's question was gentle but pointed. "From what I understand of his letter, he's simply asking you to be yourself—his colleague and, presumably, his friend. The assumption others might make is their misconception, not your deception."

Anna hadn't considered it from that angle. "I suppose that's true, but..."

"But you're afraid," *Dawdi* finished for her.

"Not afraid," she corrected quickly. "Just practical. I have other reasons I shouldn't go." She gestured to her notebook.

"May I?" He held out his hand, and reluctantly, she passed him the notebook. He scanned her list, nodding thoughtfully. "All valid concerns. And yet, you haven't declined his invitation after a week of deliberation. That suggests to me there must be compelling reasons to consider it as well."

He flipped to her second, shorter list and read it with a small smile. "Scholarly opportunities. Very practical indeed."

Anna felt her cheeks warm. "A chance to work together in person on the journal is significant."

"Of course." His eyes twinkled knowingly. "And I imagine there's nothing on this list about simple curiosity regarding this young man with whom you've been corresponding so enthusiastically."

"*Dawdi*!" Anna protested, though she couldn't quite hide a smile. "Our correspondence has been purely academic."

"As was my initial correspondence with your grandmother," he reminded her, his expression softening with memory. "We exchanged letters for nearly two years before we met in person. And when we did..." He paused, lost momentarily in recollection. "Sometimes, Anna, the most significant discoveries come when we step outside our carefully organized lives."

Anna studied her grandfather's face, seeing the tender reminiscence there. She knew the story well—how her reserved grandfather had fallen in love with her grandmother when they finally met at a conference, how their shared passion for the history of their faith had blossomed into a deep and enduring marriage. But her situation was different. Wasn't it?

"There's another factor you haven't added to either list," Dawdi said, closing the notebook and placing it gently on the desk between them. "The story within the journal itself."

Anna frowned slightly. "What about it?"

"The author of that journal left everything familiar behind to travel to a new land, facing uncertainty and risk." He gestured to the leather-bound book. "We've spent months studying her courage, her willingness to step into the unknown. Perhaps there's a lesson there beyond the historical facts."

The observation struck Anna with unexpected force. Her grandfather was right—she'd been deeply moved by the journal author's bravery in facing new circumstances, yet here she was, hesitating over a simple trip to Prince Edward Island.

"Besides," *Dawdi* continued pragmatically, "I can manage the museum for a week. Samuel Weaver's son has been asking for summer work, and this would be an excellent opportunity to train him."

"You seem awfully anxious for me to go," Anna wondered at his quick and easy acceptance of this idea when she'd been in a conundrum over it for the past week.

He smiled gently. "Your birthday is approaching, Anna. Twenty-one is a wonderful age for new experiences. I see this as an answer to my prayers for something special for you."

"Even experiences involving deceptive wedding invitations?" she asked wryly.

"Even those." He rose from his chair, placing a gentle hand on her shoulder. "The question isn't whether going is practical. The question is whether staying is what you truly want."

After her grandfather left, Anna turned back to the computer screen. Michael's email remained open, the cursor blinking in the reply field that had been empty for a week.

She flexed her fingers and typed:

Dear Michael,

Thank you for your invitation. After careful consideration, I would be pleased to attend your brother's wedding, though I feel I should clarify a few points regarding our arrangement...

As she composed her response, Anna felt a curious lightness, as if putting words to the decision had lifted some invisible weight. Perhaps, just this once, she could step outside the careful display case of her life and see what lay beyond.

Michael arrived at the one-room schoolhouse just after dawn, a full hour before the community working bee was scheduled to begin. The quiet solitude was exactly what he needed to collect his thoughts and envision the space as his classroom.

Mattie's meticulous organization helped to make the transition easier. His sister had left detailed notes about each scholar's progress and temperament, along with suggestions for the fall term. Still, the transition from Mattie's domain to his own would require time and thoughtful consideration. Even if their Amish traditions made the variation limited, a new teacher always brought a period of adjustment for everyone.

He stood at the teacher's desk, running his fingers along the smooth wooden edge. Soon, twenty-four scholars of various ages would look to him for guidance, structure and wisdom. The weight of that responsibility settled on his shoulders—not unwelcome, but substantial nonetheless.

Moving deliberately around the room, Michael mentally pictured a full classroom, calculating the optimal layout for different age groups. The youngest scholars needed closer supervision, while the older ones required independence to develop their self-discipline. He made notes in a small leather-bound notebook and listed supplies needed for the fall term.

"First male teacher in New Hope," he murmured to himself, straightening a row of readers on the bookshelf. "No pressure at all."

The sound of buggy wheels and voices outside signaled the arrival of the first volunteers. Michael took a deep breath, tucking away his notebook and preparing to shift from solitary planning to a full-fledged community working bee.

Bishop Nafzinger was the first to enter, nodding approvingly as he observed Michael already at work. "I see you've been busy already," he remarked, hanging his hat on a peg by the door. "A *goot* sign for a productive day. Soon enough, everyone will be here and ready to help."

"*Denki*, Bishop," Michael replied, grateful for the older man's supportive presence.

More church members filtered in—men carrying tools for repair work, women with cleaning supplies and fabric for new curtains. The schoolhouse quickly filled with purposeful activity and conversation.

Michael's father arrived with his younger brothers in tow. Herschel gave Michael an encouraging nod before directing Martin and Mason to help repair loose floorboards near the back of the room. And twelve-year-old Micah had been assigned to carry in buckets of whitewash for the exterior trim.

"Michael," Joel Yoder called from the doorway, "we're replacing some of the playground equipment. Your input would be appreciated."

Michael followed him outside, where several men were waiting for the go-ahead to erect a new swing-set.

"We want to make sure you still want the new swings in the same place as before," Joel continued, his voice carrying just enough for the nearby workers to hear. "There's been some concern it's too close to the softball diamond, and a suggestion has been made to move them closer to the schoolhouse."

"*Ya*, I recall an occasional fly ball coming too close to the smaller *kinner*," Michael replied, uncomfortably aware of all the attention turned in his direction. It was a feeling he knew he'd have to get used to, as he tried to answer with confidence. "I am all for moving the swings closer to the schoolhouse."

The next hour passed in productive labor, with Michael moving between inside and outside tasks, offering suggestions when asked but generally pitching in the same as everyone else.

As the morning progressed, he noticed Ada and Sarah working with a group of women in the cleaning and organization of the classroom interior. His mother had arrived as well, quietly washing windows and keeping a careful distance from the more animated discussions led by Ada and Sarah.

When Michael returned inside to check on the progress, he found himself suddenly flanked by the two women, their expressions alight with purpose.

"Such dedication to your new position," Ada began, her voice carrying a flattering tone that somehow made Michael feel like a prized bull at auction. "The *kinner* will surely benefit from your enthusiasm."

"I hope to serve them well," Michael replied neutrally, focusing on examining a loose hinge rather than meeting her gaze directly.

"My cousin's daughter, Heather, was so excited to hear about a young man taking on the teaching role," Ada continued. "She's quite interested in education herself."

"That's... nice." Michael tightened a screw with perhaps more force than necessary.

Sarah joined them, carrying a basket of cleaning rags. "Michael, we were just discussing the arrangements for Mark's wedding. I'd hate for my niece, Leah, to be left without a companion for the wedding supper."

"I'm sure Mark and Ellen will be very considerate in the seating arrangements," Michael answered, searching desperately for an escape from this conversation. They were already trying to get him to commit to sitting with one of their unmarried kinfolk.

"Of course, of course," Ada nodded. "But there will also be the singing afterward. Many opportunities to become better acquainted with our visitors."

"I've always wondered," Sarah added with calculated casualness, "what qualities you might look for in a *fraa* someday. Such a thinking man like yourself must have given it thought."

Before Michael could respond, his mother appeared at his side, her calm presence a welcome buffer.

"I think," Belinda said gently, "that Michael has always appreciated those who share his interests in history and languages. He has a mind of his own on these things."

The slight emphasis she placed on "history and languages" sent a jolt of suspicion through Michael. Had Samy said something? The knowing look in his mother's eyes suggested she knew more than she should.

"Well," Ada said, momentarily taken aback, "I'm sure many young women appreciate history and so forth."

"Indeed," Belinda agreed with a pleasant smile. "But Michael has never been one to be rushed in his decisions. When he finds the right person, I'm sure we'll all know."

The certainty in her tone only increased Michael's unease. His mother never took part in matchmaking schemes, preferring to let her children find their own paths. Yet now she seemed to hint at something—or someone—specific.

"If you'll excuse me," Michael said, seizing the moment, "I need to check on the bookshelves."

He made his way to the back of the schoolhouse where Samy had just entered. Her prayer *kapp* was slightly askew and dust from the horse barn still clung to her apron. She had clearly come directly from Noah Detweiler's farm.

"Samy," he called, perhaps too urgently. "Could you help me with the books for a moment?"

She looked up, momentarily startled from whatever thoughts had occupied her mind. "I just got here."

"Please," he added, guiding her toward the farthest bookshelf, where fewer people would notice their conversation.

Once they were reasonably secluded, Michael spoke in a low voice. "Samy, what exactly did you tell my mother about Anna?"

Samy's eyes widened slightly, but she didn't feign ignorance. "I told her and my *mamm* that you invited Anna to the wedding. That's all."

"That's all?" Michael pressed, his heart racing. "You didn't mention—"

"That you only asked her to pretend?" Samy shook her head. "*Nay.* I didn't tell them that part."

Relief washed through him, followed immediately by an additional concern. "So now they think—"

"That you're genuinely interested in her," Samy finished matter-of-factly, beginning to organize books on the shelf. "Isn't that what you wanted everyone to assume, anyway?"

Michael ran a hand over his face. "Yes, but—"

"They were pleased," Samy continued, methodically arranging readers by height. "Much better than having them think you're using someone just to avoid their plans."

The direct assessment made Michael wince. When Samy put it that way, his reasons did sound rather callous.

"Your *mamm* looked happy," Samy added. "*Aenti* Sarah and Ada probably won't be, though."

Despite his anxiety, Michael couldn't help a small smile at that. "I noticed."

They worked in silence for a moment, Samy's precise movements bringing order to the jumbled collection of books.

"*Mamm* gave me the key to the shop this morning," she said finally, without looking up. "Said she wouldn't be opening until afternoon but asked me to check her messages, in case anything needed her urgent attention."

"Oh?" Michael's fingers paused on the binding of a primer.

"Maybe you should check your email," Samy muttered. "See if Anna answered you."

His heart skipped a beat. "Did she? What did she say?"

"I promised not to read other people's email anymore. Remember?" Samy replied with dignity. "But if I were you, I'd want to know before the wedding planning gets any more advanced."

"*Denki*, Samy," he said, keeping his voice steady despite the sudden urgency he felt. "For keeping your promise and for letting me know."

She nodded, then asked with surprising directness, "Do you really want her to come?"

The question caught him off guard. "I... it's complicated."

"Most things are," Samy replied with unexpected wisdom. "But if she comes, you will be nice to her, *ya*? Don't just use her to avoid Ada's niece and Sarah's cousin."

"Anna is my friend, Samy. Of course, I will be nice to her. And don't forget that I did not mislead her. I was perfectly honest with her about my... predicament."

Samy paused, as if considering what he'd said, then continued, "The new family moved into Beulah Erb's old farmhouse yesterday. The Fishers. They have a girl my age."

The abrupt change of subject was typical Samy, but Michael was grateful for it. "That's good news," he said, then realized his mention of Anna being his friend must have prompted the change of subject.

Samy continued, her tone revealing uncharacteristic interest. "She has a rabbit. I saw her holding the cage when they arrived."

"You like rabbits?" Michael asked, suddenly unsure if it was the new girl, the rabbit, or both which interested her.

"I like all animals," Samy replied matter-of-factly. "But I've never had a rabbit. Just Amazon and the barn cats."

Michael smiled at the glimpse into Samy's inner world. "Perhaps you'll meet the new girl and her rabbit soon."

Samy nodded, then lowered her voice again as she reached for another stack of books. "You should check that email. Soon. Before your *mamm* starts planning your wedding too."

The mischief in her tone wasn't lost on Michael. "I believe you want Anna to come. Am I right?"

Samy kept at her work, either pretending not to hear him or simply ignoring the question. He chuckled, then glanced toward where his mother was speaking quietly with Lydia Yoder, both occasionally looking in his direction with expressions he couldn't quite decipher.

Whatever Anna's response might be, he needed to know before the situation grew even more complicated. The thought of disappointing his mother's newly kindled hopes for a romantic relationship troubled him, but not as much as the prospect of continuing this charade without knowing if Anna had even agreed to come.

"If you'll let me into the shop, I'll check," he promised Samy. "As soon as I'm done here later this afternoon."

"I have to leave to go work with Noah and the horses, but I'll wait for you at the *shoppe* when I'm done." Satisfied, she returned to organizing books with meticulous precision, while Michael's mind raced with possibilities. Had Anna responded? And if so, what had she decided?

Chapter Four

Barn smells were comforting—the sweet hay, leather, and the unique earthy scent of horses. Samy inhaled deeply as she entered Noah Detweiler's therapy stable. Here, the world made sense. Animals didn't expect complicated social rituals or unspoken rules. They responded honestly to how you treated them, which was much simpler than dealing with people.

"Hello, Amazon," she murmured, approaching her Morgan mare. "I'm finally back." The horse nickered softly, extending her elegant head over the half-door of the stall.

Samy ran her hand along Amazon's sleek neck, counting strokes as she always did. Twenty strokes exactly, no more and no less, a routine that mattered to them both.

"She was waiting for you," Noah's voice called from the feed room. He emerged with a bucket of grain, his tall frame slightly stooped to avoid the low doorway. "Been watching the path since you left her here earlier."

Samy nodded, not surprised.

Noah smiled beneath his beard. "And how are things at the schoolhouse for the new teacher?"

"People kept bothering him with marriage talk." Samy moved to fetch Amazon's brush from the nearby tack box. "It's silly. He's going to be a teacher. Why does everyone want him to get married right away?"

"That's just how folks are," Noah replied, distributing feed to the therapy horses. "Been the same since the beginning of time, I reckon."

Samy began brushing Amazon with precise, measured strokes. "Michael already invited someone to the wedding. A Mennonite girl from Ontario. Anna."

Noah paused. "Did he now? That's news."

"She works at a museum. They translate old journals together." Samy continued the measured brushing. "He doesn't want anyone to know he invited her, but everyone will find out soon enough."

"Sounds like you've been privy to some secrets," Noah observed, though his tone held no judgment.

"Not on purpose," Samy knew she should probably stop talking about it, but Noah was the one person outside of her family that she could trust with anything. He always listened. And he always understood. "I just happened to be there when—"

The sound of wheels on gravel interrupted her explanation. Noah glanced toward the barn entrance.

"That'll be our first appointment," he said. "Earlier than usual."

A moment later, a man Samy didn't recognize appeared at the barn entrance, guiding a boy of about eight years old by the shoulder. Behind them followed a girl approximately Samy's age, carrying something in her arms that Samy couldn't immediately identify.

"Nathan Fisher," the man introduced himself to Noah with an extended hand. "I believe Rachel was expecting us this morning for David."

"Welcome," Noah greeted them warmly. "Rachel mentioned you'd be coming. I'm Noah Detweiler. This is Samy Yoder, one of our best horse handlers."

Samy remained close to Amazon, though she observed the newcomers from the corner of her eye.

"This is David," Nathan introduced the fidgeting boy. "And my eldest, Sharon."

Samy's ears perked up at the name of the new girl with the rabbit.

Sure enough, cradled in Sharon's arms was a fawn-colored rabbit visible through the wire door. Samy's curiosity overcame her.

"Is that your rabbit?" The question burst from her lips before she could consider a proper greeting.

Sharon looked startled by the direct inquiry. "*Ya,*" she answered softly. "This is Maple."

"Why did you bring him to a horse farm?" Samy asked, practical concerns immediately surfacing. "Horses might frighten him. And he might frighten the therapy horses."

Sharon's cheeks flushed slightly, and only then did Samy realize her tone had been too blunt. A hard lump stuck in her throat. She had so looked forward to meeting Sharon and her rabbit, and now she'd ruined it.

Noah stepped in smoothly. "Sharon, why don't you take Maple to the tack room while I get David started with Buttercup? He'll be safe there, and you can help with the session if you'd like."

Sharon nodded gratefully and headed toward the tack room.

Samy felt a strange impulse to follow. She wanted to see the rabbit up close, but she was frozen in place. Unsure. Embarrassed.

"Go ahead," Noah said quietly. "You just have to get to know each other, and then things will come easier."

After a moment's hesitation, Samy set down the brush and followed Sharon into the tack room. The girl had settled on a bench and was whispering to the rabbit.

"Does he like being petted?" Samy asked, approaching cautiously.

Sharon looked up, maybe a bit surprised Samy had followed her. But then she smiled, easing Samy's worry. "*Ya*, he does. Would you like to pet him?"

Samy nodded, watching as Sharon lifted the rabbit up for her to pet it. The animal's soft fur and alert eyes immediately captivated her.

"How old is he?" Samy asked, carefully extending her hand.

"Two years," Sharon answered, demonstrating how to offer her hand for the rabbit to sniff. "I've had Maple since he was a kit."

"He's very calm," Samy observed, running a finger lightly over the rabbit's soft back.

"He's good with people," Sharon said, a note of pride in her voice. "Even with all the moving and changes, he stays calm."

The rabbit's acceptance of her touch was satisfying in a way Samy hadn't expected. "I've never had a rabbit. Just horses and barn cats," she said. "I'm Samy. Samy Yoder."

"Sharon Fisher," the girl replied, though they'd already been introduced. "We just moved into Beulah Erb's old farmhouse."

"I know," Samy said. "I saw your wagon yesterday. You were holding Maple's carrier."

Sharon looked surprised. "You saw us arrive?"

"From my kitchen window," Samy clarified. "I was washing dishes."

An awkward silence fell between them. Samy realized she should probably say something welcoming but wasn't sure what.

"Do you like horses?" she finally asked, gesturing toward the barn.

Sharon nodded, stroking Maple's ears with practiced gentleness. "I've never worked with them like this before, though."

"Noah uses horses to help people," Samy explained. "I help him with the horses. They listen to me."

"That's special," Sharon said, her voice sincere. "Not everyone can communicate well with animals."

The observation pleased Samy, though she wasn't sure how to respond to the compliment. Instead, she asked, "How many brothers and sisters do you have?"

"Five," Sharon answered. "I'm the oldest. David is here for therapy. He has... trouble sitting still sometimes."

Samy nodded. "The horses help with that. They don't like sudden movements, so people have to learn to be calm around them."

From the barn, they heard Noah calling for Sharon to join them if she wanted to see David's first session.

"You can leave Maple here," Samy said. "I'll watch him while I finish with Amazon."

Sharon hesitated, clearly protective of her pet.

"I'm good with animals," Samy assured her. "Ask Noah if you don't believe me."

After a moment's consideration, Sharon carefully placed Maple back in his carrier. "His water bottle is full, but he might get scared with the horse sounds."

"I'll talk to him," Samy promised. "Animals like it when you explain things to them."

A small smile formed on Sharon's lips. "*Ya*, they do." She glanced toward the door where Noah was calling again. "I should go see David."

"I'll be here," Samy replied, already turning her attention to the rabbit, who was watching her with bright, curious eyes.

As Sharon left, Samy thought that maybe—just maybe—having new neighbors wouldn't be such a bad thing after all. Especially if they came with interesting animals.

Michael balanced precariously on the ladder, fork in hand, tossing hay into the loft of the Beller family barn. The physical labor provided welcome relief from the morning's events at the schoolhouse. But it did little to quiet the racing of his thoughts. His mind had been in a whirl ever since he'd checked his email at Lydia's Shoppe afterward.

Anna had replied.

After the working bee concluded, Samy was waiting to unlock the door for him, just as she'd promised. She'd left him alone this time. Thankfully. And there in the quiet back corner, he had opened his email to find Anna's response waiting for him.

She was coming.

The thought sent equal measures of relief and panic coursing through him. Relief that his plan might actually work—he would have someone to deflect the matchmaking attempts at Mark's wedding. But panic at the realization of what he'd set in motion.

Anna's reply had been gracious but contained several questions about practical matters—specifically about appropriate dress for an Amish community gathering. Questions he wasn't entirely equipped to answer.

"You're missing half the loft," his father's amused voice called from below. "Something on your mind, *sohn*?"

Michael glanced down to see hay scattered across the barn floor rather than neatly piled as intended. "Sorry, *Datt*. Just distracted."

Herschel Beller studied his son with discerning eyes. "Schoolhouse preparations troubling you?"

"Not exactly," Michael replied, descending the ladder. He hesitated, then decided simple honesty was the best approach. "I've invited someone to Mark's wedding. Anna... from Ontario. She's the one I've been doing translation work with by mail."

His father's eyebrows rose slightly. "The girl from the Mennonite Museum? Your *mamm* mentioned something of the sort."

"What? How would she.." He remembered her comments to the PTA mothers and Samy's confession. Of course she had told his *datt*. Hopefully his father was the only one she'd told, but he decided he didn't even want to ask. "Never mind how she knows. What's done is done. But y*a*, I invited Anna Roth. And she's agreed to come."

This next part—what had him so distracted—was more difficult to talk about. "*Vell Datt*," Michael cleared his throat. "She asked me how she's supposed to dress while visiting here. She doesn't want to offend anyone. And well, we've never had a reason to discuss any details about our community here in New Hope. Not that kind anyway." Michael brushed his damp palms across his thighs. Talking about women's clothing wasn't something he'd ever done with anyone before.

"*Ach*, I see," his father nodded thoughtfully. "That would be a question better answered by your *mamm* or perhaps Lydia Yoder."

"I was afraid of that," Michael sighed, leaning his pitchfork against a stall.

His father's eyes crinkled with amusement. "Not comfortable discussing women's clothing, are you?"

"Not particularly," Michael admitted.

Just then, the barn door opened, and Belinda Beller entered, carrying a basket covered with a linen cloth.

"I thought you two might be hungry," his *mamm* said, setting the basket on a bale of hay. "Fresh bread and cheese."

"Perfect timing," Herschel smiled, his weathered hand reaching for his wife's briefly—a rare public display of affection that made Michael glance away.

"Michael was just telling me about his wedding guest," his father continued, accepting a piece of bread. "The young woman from Ontario."

His mother's eyes brightened. "Anna Roth. So, she *is* coming, for sure?"

Michael nodded, not missing for a second the slow smile overtaking his *mamm's* expression. He took a deep breath, trying to ignore her assumption about the situation. "*Ya*, and she's asked how to dress for visiting our community."

"Oh," Belinda considered this. "Well, she's Mennonite, isn't she? Her head covering will be different from ours, of course, but that's to be expected."

"She's concerned about causing offense," Michael explained, remembering Anna's carefully worded email. "Her community allows more colorful clothing than ours."

Belinda waved a dismissive hand. "We regularly interact with Mennonites and even *Englisch*. No one will take offense at her following her own tradition. You haven't explained this about New Hope? Seems she must be concerned we are a much stricter district than we are."

Michael shifted his weight from one foot to the other, growing more uncomfortable with each question. "*Nay*, it's not been a topic of discussion between us until now."

His *mamm's* lips pursed. "Michael, don't you think a woman ought to know at least the basics about some of these things before... before you begin courting her?"

Ya, he supposed so, but that wasn't what was really happening here. And he was hard-pressed to know how to answer his *mamm* with that disappointed look on her face.

"Anna will need a place to stay," his mother pointed out. "If we weren't already hosting so many kin from Ontario, I'd insist she stay here with us. I'll double-check with your sister, Mattie. They have a crowd of Ellen's kinfolk coming from Lancaster, still it's possible she and Winston might have room yet for one more guest." She paused, then raised a finger to her lips as she did when she had an idea. "Still, it wouldn't hurt to mention the need of a host family for Anna to Joel and Lydia."

Michael felt a twinge of guilt at putting Anna in such a predicament but reasoned he could speak with the Yoders before the day was out. Lydia was known for her hospitality, so maybe Anna could even stay with them. And Michael had a sense that Anna would be very understanding of Samy.

"I'll go speak with Joel now," he decided, setting down his pitchfork. "Anna will need an answer soon."

His *mamm* nodded approvingly. "*Goot.* Now that's what I would expect from my thoughtful *sohn.*"

Michael excused himself and headed across the fields toward the Yoder farm. Joel would likely be in his workshop at this time, crafting the furniture that supplemented the family's farming income.

As he walked, Michael mentally rehearsed his explanation. Anna was a friend. Their relationship was purely academic. Her visit was a courtesy, an opportunity to advance their translation work in person.

Yet even as he rehearsed these practical justifications, Michael found himself wondering what Anna was truly like in person. Her letters revealed an ordered mind, a precise way of thinking that he appreciated. But what would her voice sound like? Would she speak as carefully as she wrote?

Joel's workshop came into view, a small building next to the Yoder barn. The door stood open, and the rhythmic sound of planing wood carried on the summer air.

"Joel?" Michael called from the doorway. "Do you have a minute?"

Joel looked up from the cabinet he was crafting, setting his plane aside. "Michael, of course. *Kumm* inside. I'm almost done here."

Michael stepped into the workshop, appreciating its orderly arrangement. Tools hung in precise locations, wood was stacked by type and size, and sawdust was carefully swept into a corner.

"What brings you here?" Joel asked, wiping his hands on a cloth.

"I've invited a guest to Mark's wedding," Michael began. "A Mennonite friend from Ontario with whom I've been corresponding about translation work."

Joel nodded, his expression neutral. "Ah, yes. Lydia mentioned something about this. Anna Roth, correct?"

News traveled quickly in their small community. Michael winced, wondering how many more people already knew. "Yes. She's accepted my invitation, but I'm afraid I didn't think this through so well before..." Before Samy hit the send button, but he didn't say so. This was all on him, and he knew it. "For one thing, she has questions about how to dress for visiting here."

Joel considered this for a moment. "She's Mennonite. She should dress according to her own traditions. We do not expect visitors to adopt our ways temporarily."

Michael felt relief at the straightforward answer. "That's helpful. She was concerned about causing offense."

"A considerate thought," Joel acknowledged. "But unnecessary. Her modest Mennonite dress will be entirely appropriate."

Michael hesitated before adding, "There's also the matter of where she will stay. Our house is already going to be overflowing. Mattie and Winston might squeeze her in, but I was wondering if perhaps she might stay with your family? Samy could benefit from her companionship. She's a very thoughtful person with a great deal of patience. And well, the truth is that it would be convenient for our work together to have her here at your house, not far from our own and just across the street from the school."

Joel's eyebrows rose slightly. "Samy isn't too fond of sharing her room, but then her cousins who come to visit are all small children. A kind young woman whom she would respect would probably be a *goot* thing for her. I would have no objection, though I should consult with Lydia first. She may have plans I am unaware of."

"Of course," Michael agreed quickly.

Joel studied him for a moment, his expression thoughtful. "You know, Michael, I appreciate that you've chosen a Mennonite friend to accompany you. It makes things... simpler."

"Simpler?" Michael echoed.

"Indeed," Joel nodded. "No confusion about potential courtship. With her being Mennonite and you Amish, both communities understand the natural limitations. It spares you the complications of romantic expectations that might interfere with your teaching duties."

Michael felt an unexpected twist of discomfort at Joel's matter-of-fact assessment. "I hadn't thought of it quite that way."

"It's practical," Joel continued. "The bishop selected you partly because you seemed unlikely to be distracted by courtship. A Mennonite friend poses no such distraction."

Michael found himself strangely irritated by Joel's certainty. "Anna and I... well, we know each other because of our common interest in history and languages. But we are friends too."

"Exactly," Joel nodded, apparently missing the defensive note in Michael's voice. "Friends without romantic complications. Very sensible."

Before Michael could respond, Joel added, "When will she arrive?"

"Her bus from Charlottetown arrives three days before the wedding," Michael answered.

"I can speak with Dan King's son," Joel offered. "He often drives visitors since his father passed last year. He may already have a trip planned to Charlottetown due to all the visitors coming for the wedding."

"That won't be necessary," Michael replied, perhaps too quickly. "I can make arrangements to meet her myself."

Joel's expression remained neutral, though something flickered in his eyes.

Michael hurried to explain, trying to cover what had sounded like he was keen on meeting his sweetheart. "I mean, Mark is probably available to drive, and he and I need to discuss some of the wedding stuff, anyway."

"I see, then I'll speak with Lydia about the accommodations." Joel nodded his approval.

"Thank you," Michael said, preparing to leave. "Anna will appreciate your understanding on the dress matter as well."

As he walked back toward the Beller farm, Michael found himself surprisingly unsettled by the conversation. Joel's casual dismissal of any romantic potential between him and Anna should have been reassuring. After all, wasn't that the whole point? To have a companion who would deflect matchmaking without creating genuine expectations.

Yet something about Joel's certainty rankled him. As if the mere fact of their different communities made any deeper connection impossible.

The more troubling realization, however, was his own reaction. Why should he care if Joel dismissed the romantic potential? Anna was a friend, nothing more.

Wasn't she?

In seven days, he'd be standing at the Charlottetown bus station, waiting to meet Anna Roth in person for the first time. The thought sent an unexpected spark of anticipation through him—one that had nothing to do with evading matchmakers and everything to do with finally putting a face, a voice, a presence to the mind he already admired through their correspondence.

It was simply scholarly curiosity; he told himself. Nothing more.

But even as he crested the hill overlooking the Beller farm, Michael couldn't quite convince himself that was true.

C hapter Five

The gentle hum of the bus engine changed pitch as it slowed, pulling Anna's attention from her book again. Outside the window, the landscape of Prince Edward Island unfolded in a patchwork of rolling green fields, red soil and glimpses of ocean. For the past hour, she'd been too captivated by the view to focus on reading, despite bringing L.M. Montgomery's *Blue Castle* as a comforting buffer against her growing nervousness.

"Ladies and gentlemen, we are approaching Charlottetown," the driver announced. "Please ensure you have all your belongings before departing."

Anna carefully tucked the book into her handbag and straightened her head covering. The delicate white fabric felt suddenly conspicuous as she glanced around at the other passengers—tourists in casual summer attire, businesspeople in modern clothing. While her modest dress drew little attention in her home community, here it marked her as different.

What would Michael think of her appearance? She'd chosen one of her favorite dresses for the occasion—a summer green with subtle white daisies in a random pattern. Anna had almost opted for something plainer, but *Dawdi* had insisted that she didn't need to subdue her wardrobe entirely. After all, she was Mennonite, not Amish.

Finally, she had agreed. She could only be herself. A decision that became increasingly significant as the bus pulled into the station. Somewhere beyond those doors waited Michael Beller—an Amish man she knew only through letters and one particularly awkward email invitation.

The bus came to a complete stop. Around her, passengers gathered bags and jackets, creating a shuffling queue in the narrow aisle. Anna remained seated, allowing others to go ahead while she gathered her courage along with her belongings.

What had she been thinking, agreeing to this arrangement? Pretending to be someone's companion to deflect matchmaking—it sounded like something from one of the romance novels her friend Mary occasionally loaned to her to read. And she'd never read one with a heroine like herself.

"Miss? Is this your stop?" The driver's voice interrupted her spiraling thoughts.

"Yes, thank you," Anna replied, collecting her modest suitcase from the overhead compartment and making her way to the front.

The island air that greeted her was fresh and carried the distant scent of saltwater. Anna took a deep breath, allowing it to steady her as she stepped onto the platform and scanned the waiting area.

Several people stood near the entrance, but none matched what she imagined Michael might look like. Her mind had constructed a vague image based on the precise, thoughtful nature of his letters—perhaps gangly with glasses and a serious demeanor.

"Anna?"

She turned toward the voice and felt her carefully rehearsed greeting die on her lips.

The young man approaching her was not at all what she had imagined. Tall and broad-shouldered, Michael Beller moved with the easy confidence of someone accustomed to physical labor. His light brown hair was cut in the traditional Amish style, falling just below his ears beneath a straw hat. But it was his eyes that caught her attention—light brown with flecks of gold, intelligent and searching as they met hers.

"Michael," she managed, extending her hand in what she hoped was a composed gesture. "It's good to finally meet you in person."

His handshake was firm but gentle, his palm calloused from farm work yet careful in its pressure. "Welcome to Prince Edward Island. I hope your journey wasn't too tiring?"

There was a formality to his speech that reminded her of his letters, and it helped to ground her. This was indeed the same thoughtful correspondent she had come to know, regardless of his unexpected appearance.

"Not at all," she replied, gathering her composure. "The scenery was worth every mile."

An elderly woman behind Anna struggled with a heavy bag, and without hesitation, Anna turned to help, steadying the bag while the woman found her balance.

"Thank you, dear," the woman smiled gratefully. "So kind of you."

Anna returned the smile. "Of course. Safe travels."

When she turned back to Michael, she found him watching her with an expression she couldn't quite decipher—something between surprise and approval.

"You must be hungry after your journey," he said, gesturing toward the station exit. "There's a Tim Hortons nearby. We could get something before heading to New Hope, if you'd like."

The thoughtfulness of the offer touched her. He could have rushed her straight to the Yoders' house but instead considered her comfort first. She could use a little chance to adjust before her first meeting of New Hope's minister and his family. Although she was quite interested in meeting Samy, the young girl Michael had mentioned in his last email.

"That would be lovely and is very thoughtful of you," she replied. "Thank you."

A hint of color touched his cheeks at the compliment. "It's the least I could do, considering... well, considering everything."

The unspoken reference to his unusual invitation hung briefly between them before Anna made an effort to put them both at ease.

"There's so much for us to talk about," she said with a small smile, "but perhaps over coffee rather than in the middle of a bus station?"

His expression relaxed visibly and smiled. "*Ya*. Talking is always better with a donut and *kaffi*."

As they walked toward the exit, Anna carrying her smaller bag while Michael insisted on taking her suitcase, she felt some of her anxiety recede. Whatever complications this visit might bring, at least Michael Beller seemed to be exactly what his letters had suggested—thoughtful, considerate, and refreshingly straightforward.

Now she just had to navigate the delicate matter of pretending to be his companion without actually becoming attached to him. Given the religious differences that stood firmly between them, that should be simple enough.

Shouldn't it?

Michael watched Anna as she carefully added a precise amount of cream to her coffee, her movements deliberate and graceful. Everything about her spoke of order and thoughtfulness—from the neat arrangement of her belongings to the careful way she worded her responses.

He had expected someone bookish, perhaps severe in demeanor. Instead, Anna Roth possessed a quiet grace that surprised him. Her pretty dress complemented her hazel-green eyes that shifted between light and dark in the light. Beneath her Mennonite-style head covering, he glimpsed brown hair with hints of auburn. But it was her composure that impressed him most—the way she had helped the elderly woman without hesitation, how she politely thanked the café server, her ability to put him immediately at ease despite the awkwardness of their situation.

"Your home is quite far from Charlottetown?" she asked, bringing the coffee cup to her lips.

"About an hour's drive by car. Too far for horse and buggy," Michael replied, grateful for the neutral topic rather than how they were going to navigate the awkward situation he'd created. "My brother Mark is running errands in town. He'll join us shortly to drive us back to New Hope."

Anna nodded. "You mentioned in your letters that several of your brothers still live at home?"

"Yes," Michael confirmed. "Five brothers besides Mark, who's about to get married. He left home years ago and joined the RCAF, but he's back now. He's built a house for himself and Ellen and her little boy near our farm. But they belong to a Mennonite church. Our sister Mattie, who's his twin, is married to Winston Miller. They run a maple farm nearby. Winston's from Lancaster, and Mark's bride Ellen is his cousin."

"A large family," Anna observed with a smile, absorbing all the information about his relatives. "I'm an only child myself. The museum often feels quiet in comparison to what you must be accustomed to."

Michael couldn't imagine such solitude. The Beller household was perpetually filled with voices, movement and activity. "Do you prefer the quiet?"

"I've grown accustomed to it," she replied thoughtfully. "Though I admit, I sometimes wonder what having siblings might have been like."

"Chaotic," Michael said with a small smile. "But never boring."

"It must have prepared you for a one-room schoolhouse, for sure." Her gentle smile and affirmation made his heart flip in an unfamiliar way.

A comfortable silence fell between them as they sipped their coffee. Michael found himself studying her hands—slender fingers that handled her cup with precision, nails trimmed short and practical. Hands that had carefully transcribed the journal passages they'd been working on together, forming the neat handwriting he'd come to recognize.

"I should apologize," he said suddenly, the words escaping before he could reconsider.

Anna looked up, her expression questioning.

"For my invitation. I mean, for the awkwardness of it," he clarified, keeping his voice low despite the busy café around them. "It was... a lot of pressure for me to put on you with such short notice."

To his surprise, a small smile touched her lips. "It was certainly unexpected."

"Samy shouldn't have sent it," Michael admitted. "I was still debating whether to send it at all when she accidentally clicked the mouse."

"Ah," Anna's eyes brightened with understanding. "That explains the abrupt ending."

Michael felt heat rise in his cheeks. "I'm sorry for putting you in this position. You must think terribly of me."

"Not at all," she replied, her tone measured but kind. "I find your honesty refreshing."

Her gracious response eased some of his guilt. "You're very understanding."

"Perhaps," she conceded. "Or perhaps I'm curious about the wedding and excited to work with you on the journal in person."

The reference to their shared work immediately shifted the atmosphere. Michael felt himself on firmer ground. "I've made some progress with the passages you sent last month. The dialect has some interesting variations from standard Ukrainian."

Anna leaned forward, her eyes alight with intellectual curiosity. "I suspected as much. The syntax patterns suggested a regional variation."

Just like that, they fell into the familiar rhythm of their academic correspondence, comparing notes on translation challenges and historical context. Michael gestured with increasing animation as they discussed a difficult passage, and Anna produced a small notebook from her bag, jotting down his observations with quick, precise movements of her pen.

It was only when he noticed the café had emptied that Michael realized how much time had passed. "I should check if Mark has arrived," he said, reluctantly breaking their enthusiastic discussion.

As if summoned by the mention of his name, his brother appeared at the café entrance. Mark Beller spotted them immediately and approached with the confident stride Michael had always envied in his older brother.

"So, you're the famous Anna Roth," Mark said by way of greeting, extending his hand. "Michael mentioned your work together, but he has told us little else."

Michael felt a flash of irritation at his brother's pointed comment, but Anna merely smiled and shook Mark's hand.

"A pleasure to meet you," she said. "And congratulations on your upcoming wedding."

"Denki," Mark replied, switching effortlessly between *Englisch* and German as many who grew up Amish did. "Ellen is looking forward to meeting you. Few people capture my brother's attention the way your letters have."

Michael cleared his throat. "We should be going. It's a long drive."

"Not so far, or at least it won't feel so far as it would by buggy," Mark agreed, though his knowing smile suggested the conversation was far from over. "I parked around the side of the building to avoid the buses."

Anna looked surprised. "So, we won't be traveling by horse and buggy? I thought—"

"Mark drives," Michael explained quickly. "They allow cars in the Mennonite church he joined when he returned from... his time away."

A flash of understanding crossed Anna's features. She nodded without pressing for details, another sign of her tactful nature.

As they gathered their belongings and headed toward the exit, Michael found himself acutely aware of Anna walking beside him. Their earlier discussion had momentarily allowed him to forget the uncomfortable circumstances of her visit. Now, with Mark's knowing glances and the looming introduction to the rest of his family and the community, reality crashed back upon him.

What had he been thinking, inviting her here? The plan had seemed straightforward when considered abstractly—have Anna attend the wedding as his guest, deflect matchmaking attempts, then part ways afterward. But Anna Roth wasn't an abstract solution to his problem. She was a real person with her own life, her own feelings.

A real person who had just traveled hundreds of miles based on his impulsive invitation.

A real person, he might like even more in person than through her letters.

Outside at Mark's truck—a rather large one at that—Anna hesitated briefly at the height of the step up to the cab. Michael offered his hand to help her climb in, an instinctive gesture that resulted in a moment of unexpected connection as her fingers grasped his.

"Thank you," she said softly, settling onto the seat.

As Michael took his place beside her, with Mark climbing in the driver's side, he was struck by the realization that they would now need to maintain their pretense in earnest. The abstract had become concrete, and a bead of sweat formed along his forehead.

"Ready for New Hope?" Mark asked, glancing at them with a barely concealed smirk.

Michael nodded, casting a sidelong glance at Anna. Her profile was serene as she gazed at the Charlottetown streets passing by, but her hands in her lap betrayed a slight tension in their careful stillness.

"Yes," Michael answered for them both, uncertain whether he spoke truth or wishful thinking. "We're ready."

Later that evening after all the travel and introductions to so many new people, including Lydia and Joel, who graciously opened their home to her for her stay, Anna felt as if she could fall asleep standing up. What a day it had been, she mused as she followed Samy up the stairs of the Yoder's farmhouse to her room.

"You can have the bed by the window," Samy announced as she led Anna into the bedroom they would share. The room was simply furnished but tidy, with two narrow beds, a small dresser and a desk beneath the window. A kerosene lamp cast a warm glow over the polished wooden floors.

"Thank you," Anna replied, setting her suitcase at the foot of the indicated bed. "It's a lovely room."

Samy nodded, satisfied with the arrangement. "I put fresh sheets on this morning. And I moved my rock collection, so you'd have space for your things." She gestured to the desk where a carefully arranged display of stones had been pushed to one side.

"That's very kind of you," Anna said, touched by the girl's thoughtfulness.

The evening had passed in a blur of introductions and conversation. Lydia Yoder had welcomed her warmly, immediately making Anna feel at home with her gentle hospitality. Joel, though more reserved, had been equally welcoming, asking thoughtful questions about her grandfather's museum and their translation work.

Michael had stayed for supper, sitting across from Anna at the Yoders' large table, occasionally catching her eye with a small smile that made her heart flutter in a most unsettling way. He'd left shortly afterward, promising to return the following day to show her around New Hope.

Now, as the household settled for the night, Anna found herself alone with Samy for the first time.

"You should know," Samy said abruptly as she changed into her nightgown behind a privacy screen, "that Ada and Sarah have big plans for the wedding."

Anna paused in unpacking her nightclothes. "What kind of plans?"

"Matchmaking," Samy replied matter-of-factly, emerging in a simple white nightgown. "For Michael."

"Ah," Anna nodded, unsurprised by the information but amused with how Samy shared it. "With their nieces?"

"Leah and Heather," Samy confirmed, climbing onto her bed and folding her legs beneath her. "Leah is Ada's niece. She's nineteen and teaches Sunday school in her district in Ontario. Heather is Sarah's husband's cousin's daughter. She makes quilts and sells them in a shop."

The precision of Samy's information made Anna smile. "You seem very well-informed."

Samy shrugged. "People talk. I listen." She braided her long red hair with practiced movements. "They don't know you're coming. Or they didn't when I last heard them plotting."

"Plotting?" Anna echoed, slipping behind the screen to change.

"They have it all arranged," Samy continued, her voice lowering conspiratorially. "Leah will help with the set-up, so Michael will be sure to have to work alongside her. And Heather will be a server at the luncheon, and they'll make sure she serves Michael, all to see who he might want to sit with him at supper. They even have it in their minds that he will sit with one at supper and the other at the Singing afterward."

Anna emerged in her nightgown, trying not to smile at Samy's dramatic tone. "That sounds very... thorough."

"It's silly," Samy declared. "Michael doesn't want either of them. That's why he invited you." She paused, looking momentarily uncertain. "Isn't it?"

The direct question caught Anna off guard. "I... well, yes. That was the arrangement."

Samy nodded, satisfied. "I told him it wasn't a good idea to pretend. But I'm glad you came, anyway." She turned down her covers and slipped beneath them. "It's nice having someone here who likes books and learning things and isn't just chasing a boyfriend."

Anna took that as a compliment. "Thank you, Samy. I'm glad to be here too."

"Michael likes having you here," Samy added, matter-of-factly. "I can tell."

"Oh?" Anna tried to keep her tone neutral as she turned down her own covers.

"He smiles differently when he looks at you. Not like when he's being polite to Ada and Sarah." Samy yawned widely. "Amazon liked you too."

The abrupt change of subject was startling until Anna remembered Amazon was Samy's horse, whom she'd briefly met before supper.

"I'm honored," Anna replied with a smile. "She's a beautiful mare."

"She's the best horse," Samy agreed, her voice growing drowsy. "Tomorrow I'll show you Noah's therapy farm. The horses help people who need... help." Her words were slurring with approaching sleep. "And maybe Sharon will be there with Maple..."

Within minutes, Samy's breathing had deepened into the steady rhythm of sleep. Anna extinguished the lamp and lay back in her bed, gazing up at the ceiling where moonlight cast patterns through the curtains.

The day had been full of surprises, beginning with Michael himself. The scholarly correspondent she knew through letters had materialized as a kind man whose quiet intelligence was matched by an equally appealing personality. His genuine concern for her comfort, his animated enthusiasm when discussing their translation work, the way his eyes crinkled slightly at the corners when he smiled—all of it had caught her off guard.

More surprising still was how quickly she'd felt at ease with the Yoder family. There was a warmth to their household that reminded her of time spent with her parents before they'd left for their mission work, a sense of belonging that she'd missed without fully realizing it. The Yoders had welcomed her not as a visitor or even a guest, but almost as family.

Anna turned on her side, watching Samy's peaceful form in the adjacent bed. This arrangement was meant to be friendly—a practical solution to Michael's matchmaking dilemma and an opportunity to work together on their translation. She was to play a role, nothing more. The church community differences between them created a natural boundary that seemed insurmountable. She was Mennonite, he was Amish. Any real relationship would require one of them to leave their faith community—a sacrifice neither could reasonably ask of the other.

Yet as she drifted toward sleep, Anna wondered if those boundaries were truly as concrete as she'd assumed. The differences between their communities suddenly seemed less significant than the connection she'd felt sitting across from Michael at dinner, discussing a challenging translation passage while Joel and Lydia looked on with amusement and affection.

Tomorrow, they'd spend the day together exploring New Hope. The thought sent an unexpected thrill through her that had nothing to do with old journals or translations.

She wouldn't have to pretend at all when her feelings were already veering dangerously toward the real thing. But what would happen when it was time to return to Ontario, to her quiet life at the museum with her grandfather?

Anna pulled the quilt closer around her shoulders, listening to the unfamiliar sounds of the Yoder household settling for the night. Her visit to the island already seemed like it was going to be far too short. Then she would return home, back to her orderly, predictable life.

She'd rather have more time to truly experience this community and all it had to offer.

C hapter Six

Anna woke to the soft sounds of pre-dawn activity—quiet footsteps in the hallway, the distant clatter of cookware, a door opening and closing. For a moment, disorientation clouded her mind before she remembered: the Yoder home, New Hope, Prince Edward Island.

Michael.

Beside her, Samy's bed was already empty, the covers pulled neatly into place. The girl must rise early, probably to help with chores or visit her horse. Anna glanced at the small clock on the bedside table—5:30 a.m. Earlier than she typically did at home, but she didn't want to appear lazy to her hosts.

She dressed quickly in a simple lavender dress with a darker purple apron, arranging her prayer covering carefully over her hair. Her head covering was smaller and more delicate than the Amish ones she'd seen the women wearing yesterday but still marked her as a woman of their shared Anabaptist faith.

As she made her way downstairs, the scent of fresh bread and coffee guided her to the kitchen, where Lydia Yoder stood by the stove, stirring a large pot of oatmeal. The woman looked up with a warm smile.

"*Goot Mariye*, Anna. I hope you slept well?"

"Very well, thank you," Anna replied, hovering in the doorway. "May I help with anything?"

"You could set the table if you'd like," Lydia suggested, gesturing to a stack of plates on the counter. "Joel and the boys will be in from chores soon."

Anna moved efficiently around the kitchen, finding silverware and cups in places that seemed logical—not so different from her *dawdi's* kitchen at home. As she worked, she found herself drawn into easy conversation with Lydia about morning routines and household management.

"Samy mentioned you work at your grandfather's museum?" Lydia asked, removing freshly baked bread from the oven.

"Yes, for the past five years," Anna confirmed. "It's a small Mennonite history center and museum—just the two of us, really, with a part-time business manager who handles the financial aspects."

Lydia nodded. "Not unlike my shop. Small, but it keeps me busy." She glanced at Anna with a hint of curiosity in her eyes. "Michael mentioned he's been helping you with translation work?"

"We've been corresponding about a nineteenth-century journal," Anna explained, unsure how much Lydia knew about their work together. "It's written in several Eastern European languages, which has made it a challenge to interpret, but Michael's language interests have been a wonderful help."

"He's always been a quick learner when it comes to languages," Lydia observed, stirring the oatmeal thoughtfully. "Joel and I were pleased when he agreed to become the schoolteacher. It's good to see his gifts put to use serving the community."

Anna nodded, unsure how to respond. The unspoken question of her relationship with Michael seemed to hover between them, but Lydia didn't address it directly.

Anna wouldn't either, she decided. "I hope my visit isn't disruptive. Everyone has been very kind, and I don't mean to be a burden."

"Not at all," Lydia assured her. "It's a blessing to have you here. Samy especially seems pleased to have you share her room."

As if summoned by the mention of her name, Samy appeared at the back door, her prayer *kapp* loose and wisps of red hair escaping around her face.

"Amazon is favoring her right front leg," she announced without preamble. "I told Noah I'd be late this morning."

Lydia nodded, accepting this abrupt report. "Wash up for breakfast. Your father and brothers will be in shortly."

Samy turned to Anna, her direct gaze assessing. "Did you sleep well? Sometimes owl hoots keep visitors awake."

"I slept very well," Anna assured her. "I didn't hear any owls."

"*Goot.*" Samy nodded decisively. "Michael is coming after breakfast to show you New Hope. He said so yesterday."

The matter-of-fact statement brought a flush to Anna's cheeks that she hoped neither Lydia nor Samy would notice. "Yes, he mentioned that."

The back door opened again, admitting Joel and his two sons, Owen and young Paul, all three washing up at the sink before taking their seats at the table. Anna quickly found herself incorporated into the family breakfast routine, passing plates and pouring coffee as if she'd done so a hundred times before.

Joel offered a brief prayer of thanks, and conversation flowed easily around the table—talk of farm tasks, Samy's horse, community matters. Anna relaxed into the familiar rhythm of family life, something she hadn't experienced since her parents' divorce years ago. They'd both abandoned her to be raised by her grandfather, which, all things considered, was likely for the best. She and *Dawdi* made a happy family, but there were only two of them. It wasn't the same as what she was experiencing here with the Yoders.

"Will you be visiting the school today?" Joel asked, addressing Anna directly. "Michael has been working hard to prepare for the fall term."

Michael hadn't invited her to the schoolhouse, so Anna replied, "I wouldn't want to interfere with his work. I believe he will come here later when he's ready to show me around."

Joel nodded with approval. "I'm glad you understand his need to remain committed to his work."

"I'm sure he'd welcome the company," Lydia interjected with a knowing smile that reminded her uncomfortably of the underlying reason for Michael's invitation.

Joel's brows came together with a look of concern, or perhaps bewilderment, and the weight of the pretense she'd undertaken suddenly felt heavier. These kind people had welcomed her into their home based on a misunderstanding. Or was it? Even Anna wasn't sure exactly what was happening between her and Michael.

"I hear you run a museum with your grandfather," Joel continued. "Perhaps you could offer suggestions for the school's history display. Michael mentioned wanting to create one for the students."

"I'd be happy to," Anna said, grateful for the shift to more comfortable territory.

As breakfast concluded and the family dispersed to their various tasks, Lydia invited Anna to help in her shop before Michael arrived.

"I could use an extra pair of hands arranging merchandise," she explained. "If you don't mind?"

"Not at all," Anna replied, genuinely pleased to be useful. "I do similar work at the museum."

The small shop adjoined the Yoder's barn with a roadside public front, while also accessible through a connecting door to the traditional half of the barn. Inside Lydia's Amish Shoppe, shelves and display tables held an assortment of handcrafted items—quilts, woodwork, even some preserves. Mostly though, the shop was filled with bolts of fabric and everything one would ever need for sewing or quilting. Then Anna noticed a corner nook with bookshelves, a magazine rack and two comfortable chairs in front of a small fireplace.

"*Ach*, how lovely, Lydia. This is a place I'd feel right at home."

"*Denki*. It keeps me busy for sure, but once in a while I get to relax and read over in the corner. And some of my regular customers like to sit and browse a magazine or read a book. If I'm not too busy, we can have a cup of tea and chat." Lydia replied, handing Anna a box of newly arrived knitting needles and yarn. "These need pricing and arranging on that shelf, if you wouldn't mind."

As they worked side by side, Anna found herself drawn into a comfortable conversation with Lydia about the challenges of small business management. The parallels to the museum operation were many, and Anna shared techniques she'd developed for tracking visitor interests.

"You have a good mind for business," Lydia observed approvingly. "Similar to Michael's sister Mattie. She has a head for numbers."

"The museum requires a balance of historical knowledge and practical management," Anna explained. "My grandfather handles most of the historical aspects, while I've taken on more of the operational responsibilities."

"A good partnership," Lydia nodded. "Like Joel and myself. Different strengths coming together. It's important in a business relationship but in a marriage too. I think young people would be wise to consider that when choosing a partner for life."

The observation hung in the air, and Anna wondered if Lydia was making a subtle comment about her and Michael. Before she could decide how to respond, the shop door opened, and Michael himself entered.

His appearance shouldn't have affected her so strongly—she'd spent hours with him just yesterday. Yet the sight of him standing in the doorway, morning light catching in his hair, sent an unexpected flutter through her chest.

"Good morning," he greeted them both, though his eyes lingered on Anna. "I hope I'm not interrupting."

"Not at all," Lydia assured him. "Anna has been a *wunderbar* help."

"I'm not surprised," Michael said with a warm smile that made Anna's cheeks heat. "She's remarkably efficient in everything she does."

The compliment pleased her more than it should have. "Are you ready to show me New Hope?" she asked, setting aside the price tags she'd been working with.

"If you can spare her, Lydia?" Michael looked to his hostess.

"Of course," Lydia replied. "Anna, thank you for your help this morning. You've been a blessing."

The genuine appreciation in Lydia's voice made Anna feel both touched and guilty. Lydia saw her as Michael's special friend, perhaps even a potential courtship interest despite the religious differences. The deception, however well-intentioned, felt increasingly uncomfortable.

Yet as she joined Michael outside in the bright morning sunshine, Anna couldn't deny the genuine connection she felt—not just to him, but to this place and these people. Something about New

Hope, about the Yoders, about Michael himself, felt unexpectedly right.

And that realization was perhaps the most unsettling of all.

Later that afternoon, Michael returned to the schoolhouse. Mostly to pass the time before he was to go get Anna for supper with his family. He'd been excused from evening milking chores for that very purpose, but he'd gotten there ahead of time and didn't want to arrive at the Yoders too soon. So, he slipped into the schoolhouse, just across the way from the Yoders, to pass the extra half-hour. He was mopping the schoolroom floor with methodical strokes, enjoying the quiet of the empty building. His tour of New Hope with Anna that morning had ended at the Detweilers' farm, where Samy had eagerly shown off Amazon and introduced Anna to Noah's therapy horses. Michael had reluctantly left Anna there, promising to collect her later for supper at the Beller farm.

He had just finished wringing out the mop and setting it to dry outside when a buggy pulled into the parking area. None other than Sarah Erb and Ada Gingerich emerged. Michael suppressed a sigh.

"Michael," Sarah greeted him with a bright smile. "How refreshing to see a teacher so dedicated. Imagine our surprise to find you here."

"*Denki*, I was just about to be on my way," he replied, setting the broom aside and intentionally omitting where he was headed next.

"We won't keep you long," Ada assured him, though her expression suggested otherwise. "We were just passing by, and we must be on our way shortly as well. There are so many visitors arriving soon!"

Not missing the hint about the direction this was about to take, Michael braced himself for what would follow.

"My niece Leah arrives tomorrow," Sarah continued, her tone deliberately casual. "Albert's eldest daughter—you remember her from church gatherings when she was younger? She's grown into such a lovely young woman."

"And my cousin's daughter Heather will be here the following day," Ada added. "Such a talented girl—her quilting has won prizes at the Ontario fairs."

"How nice," Michael managed, searching for a way to redirect the conversation. "I'm sure Mark and Ellen appreciate having so many friends and family attend their celebration."

Sarah exchanged a meaningful glance with Ada. "We thought perhaps you might help us arrange some activities for the young people before the wedding. A volleyball game, perhaps? The schoolyard would be a perfect location."

The suggestion was transparent in its intent. Before Michael could formulate a diplomatic response, another buggy pulled up.

As much as Michael loved his sister Mattie, he'd never been so grateful to see her. She emerged from her buggy looking determined, which he hoped was a good sign. "Hello, Michael," she said, then nodded to the other women. "Sarah, Ada—how nice to see you both."

"I suppose you've come to check on your brother. Must be strange giving up your classroom after so many years." Sarah seemed to be making an attempt to be polite, though her smile had flipped upside down.

"Oh no, not at all. I have every confidence in my *bruder*." Mattie gave his arm a squeeze, then turned back to Sarah and Ada with wide eyes. "Have you heard the *goot* news? I've just been to see our *mamm*, and she told me that Michael has invited a special guest for the wedding. Anna Roth arrived yesterday from Ontario."

The surprised expressions on both women's faces would have been comical under other circumstances.

"A guest?" Ada repeated, her voice rising slightly.

"*Ya*, a lovely young Mennonite woman," Mattie continued pleasantly. "She works with her *dawdi* at a museum. She and Michael have been corresponding for some time."

Sarah's lips pressed into a thin line. "How... interesting. You didn't mention this, Michael."

He cleared his throat. "It didn't come up."

"She's staying with the Yoders," Mattie added. "In fact, Michael's bringing her to supper this evening." His sister turned to face him, mischief glistening in her eyes. She found this all very amusing, apparently. "That's why I was driving by at just this moment. I need to go let Winston know. *Mamm* invited us too."

The news clearly caught both women off guard. Ada recovered first, her expression smoothing into a polite smile. "Well, how... nice. We look forward to meeting her."

"Perhaps she would enjoy joining the activities we were discussing," Sarah suggested, though her enthusiasm seemed forced. "Leah and Heather would surely welcome her."

Michael could imagine few things more awkward than Anna being subjected to the scrutiny of two disappointed matchmakers and their eligible relatives. "Anna will probably be quite busy with the translation work we've planned, as will I," he said firmly. "But thank you for the thought."

An uncomfortable silence followed before Mattie spoke again. "I should go, so we won't be late for supper. Sarah, Ada—I'll see you both at the wedding, *ya?*"

The deft change of subject allowed the other two women to exit gracefully as he walked his sister to her buggy. Once they were gone, Michael turned to Mattie with an expression of profound gratitude.

"You're a lifesaver, big sister."

Mattie's light laughter eased his tension. "I thought you might appreciate some reinforcement when I saw them from the road."

Michael ran a hand over his face. "I don't understand why they're so persistent about this matchmaking."

"They want what they think is best for you, even if their methods are... somewhat misguided." She paused, studying him. "*Mamm* says Anna is lovely. I hope you know how much you have raised her hopes." She gave him a pointed look. "Hopes that you mean to do more than translation work, you know. How do you feel about all of this? About her?"

Michael wasn't sure how to respond. His mother clearly believed there was genuine potential between him and Anna, which wasn't the case. Or at least, it hadn't been when he'd invited her.

"She is," he said finally. "Smart, intelligent, thoughtful."

"And pretty?" Mattie teased, though it was clearly just a very *goot* guess.

Michael felt heat rise in his cheeks. "That's not—I mean, yes, she is, but that's not why..."

Mattie patted his arm. "It's all right, Michael. I'm happy you've found someone who shares your interests. Just don't miss what *Gott* has for you by overthinking it." She gestured to the buggy. "I'd best get going. And I look forward to meeting Anna soon."

Alone again, Michael was left with the uncomfortable realization that his deception had now spread beyond what he'd intended. His mother clearly hoped for something genuine between him and Anna, while Joel assumed their different churches made romance impossible. Or at least unlikely.

And what did Michael himself hope for? The question troubled him as he returned to his classroom preparations. Having Anna here in person was proving more complicated than he'd expected—not because of any difficulty on her part, but because of his own unexpected reactions to her presence.

Teaching. He needed to focus on teaching. That was his calling, his purpose in the community. Whatever confusion Anna's visit was causing would surely pass once she returned to Ontario after the wedding.

Three more days. Just three days, and then life would return to normal.

Michael straightened a row of readers on the shelf with more force than necessary, trying to ignore the hollow feeling that accompanied the thought of Anna's departure.

C hapter Seven

The afternoon sun cast long shadows across the path as Michael and Anna walked from the Yoders' farm toward the Beller homestead. Anna had changed from her morning dress into a deep green one with black trim, her prayer covering freshly arranged over her neatly pinned hair.

"Your family won't mind my different style of dress?" she asked, a note of concern in her voice.

"Not at all," Michael assured her. "Joel already explained that you should follow your own traditions. No one expects you to adopt our Amish ways for a brief visit." A brief visit. He lamented the words even as he said them. What, he wondered, would it be like to have Anna here for much longer?

She only nodded, seemingly relieved and totally unaware of his pondering. "I wanted to be respectful."

"The thought itself is respect enough," he replied, relieved she hadn't guessed his thoughts and touched by her consideration.

They walked in comfortable silence for a moment, accompanied only by the sounds of their footsteps on the packed earth and the distant lowing of cattle in nearby fields. Michael found himself hyperaware of Anna beside him—the subtle flowery scent that complemented her, the graceful way she moved, the thoughtful expression on her face as she observed the surrounding landscape.

"It's such a beautiful island," she said finally. "I can see why your community chose this place."

"It was Joel's vision," Michael explained. "He felt called to establish a new settlement here on the island. My family joined a few years after the first families arrived."

"From Ontario, correct?" Anna asked. "I heard, of course, about the families moving. They weren't so far from my own area."

"*Ya*, that's true, though there are differences between our districts even in Ontario," Michael said. "The Ordnung varies somewhat from place to place."

"Similar to Mennonite communities," Anna observed. "Even within the same broad tradition, practices differ."

The comparison highlighted both their similarities and their differences. Michael considered, not for the first time, the practical implications of their different faiths. A Mennonite and an Amish person could converse easily enough, worship the same God, even share many values—but belonging to different communities created a natural separation.

"I should be straightforward about something," Michael said suddenly, the words emerging before he'd fully considered them. "My mother believes there might be... romantic potential between us."

Anna's steps faltered slightly, though her expression remained composed. "I see."

"I haven't corrected her assumption," Michael continued, feeling the need to be honest. "Which isn't entirely fair to you."

"Nor to her," Anna pointed out gently. "Still, we knew this would happen, didn't we? But somehow in reality it's much more complicated than when we decided merely on paper to do this... this charade."

"*Ya*," Michael agreed, guilt washing through him. "It's become more complicated than I expected. Joel is confident that our community differences make any romance unlikely, while my mother seems hopeful despite that obstacle."

Anna was quiet for a moment; her eyes fixed on the path ahead. "And what do you believe, Michael?"

The direct question caught him off guard. "I... I'm not sure anymore," he admitted. "When I invited you, it seemed a simple solution to a practical problem. But having you here in person is..."

"Different?" she supplied when he trailed off.

"Exactly," he agreed, unable to articulate the confusion of emotions her presence had stirred.

They walked in silence for several paces before Anna spoke again. "Perhaps we should simply focus on the present—enjoying this visit, working on our translation, getting to know each other better in person. Whatever assumptions others make, we know the truth of our situation."

This plan was what Michael would have expected from their correspondence—wise and logical, like Anna herself. Yet he sensed a guarded quality to her words, as if she too was navigating uncertain feelings.

"That seems the best way forward," he agreed, though part of him wanted to press further, to understand what she truly thought about their situation.

The Beller farmhouse came into view, a large white two-story structure with a broad porch and several outbuildings. Smoke curled from the kitchen chimney, and figures moved about the yard—his brothers doing evening chores, his mother likely busy preparing supper.

"It looks like a wonderful home," Anna observed.

"It's usually quite chaotic," Michael warned her with a smile. "Five brothers still at home, plus my parents. You might regret agreeing to this meal."

"I was an only child." She laughed softly, the sound warming something inside him. "But I have always wondered what a big family would be like. I suppose you are about to show me."

As they approached the house, Michael's younger brothers noticed their arrival. Mason and Micah abandoned their chores to race toward them, curiosity clear on their faces.

"You must be Anna," Mason said without preamble. "Michael says you're very *schmart*."

"And you even know Polish," Micah added, studying her with unabashed interest. "And you work at a museum."

Anna smiled at their direct approach. "That's right. Though I'm still learning both languages."

"Boys," Michael admonished, "let Anna at least reach the house before you begin interrogating her."

"It's all right," Anna assured him. "I don't mind questions."

Her calm manner with his brothers relieved some of Michael's tension. He'd worried about how she would receive his family's inevitable curiosity, but Anna seemed perfectly comfortable with their forthright interest.

As they reached the porch, Belinda appeared at the door, wiping her hands on her apron. Her face brightened at the sight of them.

"Anna! Welcome to our home," she greeted warmly. "Come in, come in. Supper is nearly ready."

Michael watched as his mother ushered Anna inside, already engaging her in conversation about her journey and what she'd seen of the island so far. The natural way Anna fit into the household scene struck him forcefully—as if she belonged there, as if her presence filled a space he hadn't realized was empty.

Inside, the house was alive with activity. Herschel rose from his chair by the fireplace to greet their guest with dignified warmth. Myles and Martin appeared from the wash room, their hair still damp from cleaning up after chores. The younger boys peppered Anna with questions about the museum and all about Ontario, a place they'd left when too young to remember.

Throughout it all, Anna maintained a graciousness that impressed Michael deeply. She answered questions thoughtfully, asked her own with genuine interest, and complimented his mother's home with sincerity rather than empty politeness.

When they finally sat down for the meal, Michael watched Anna across the table, noting how her eyes lit up when she described the journal translation, how she gently drew out his quieter brothers with well-placed questions, and how naturally she took part in the family discussion.

"Anna was telling me she helps manage her *dawdi's* museum," Belinda remarked as she passed a plate of bread. "Quite a responsibility for someone so young."

"*Dawdi's* health isn't what it once was," Anna explained. "Taking on more of the business side of things allows him to focus on the part of the work he loves most."

"Much like Michael taking over teaching from Mattie," Herschel observed. "Allowing her to focus on the maple farm with Winston and giving Michael a purpose that is suited to his talents. *Gott* gifts each of us differently for a reason."

The parallel hadn't occurred to Michael before, but he saw its truth immediately. Both he and Anna had assumed responsibilities that enabled others to pursue their passions, while finding fulfillment of their own.

"Do you miss Ontario?" Myles asked suddenly. "Being away from your home and community?"

"I miss my grandfather, of course," Anna replied thoughtfully. "But there's something special about Prince Edward Island that makes it easy to feel at home here, even for a visitor."

Michael noted a fleeting shadow in her eyes. For all her apparent comfort with his family, Anna remained conscious of her status as a visitor—someone who would soon return to her own community, her own life. Soon.

As the meal progressed, Michael grew increasingly aware of his mother's hopeful glances, his father's thoughtful observation, and his brothers' unsubtle interest in Anna. The weight of their assumptions—that Anna might be someone special in Michael's life—unexpectedly increased his own hopes. Hopes he hadn't known he'd had, but surely he must have. How had he been so unaware of these feelings for Anna until now? Because such powerful emotions couldn't happen so quickly, could they? Somehow, he simply hadn't realized it before.

"Anna has been helping Lydia in her shop this morning," Michael mentioned, attempting to steer the conversation to safer—less personal—things. "She has excellent ideas for a new merchandise display to attract customers."

"Is that something you do at the museum?" Belinda asked. "I suppose you'd have more window shoppers in a town, though."

"That's true," Anna agreed. "But using the windows to grab customers' attention right away can increase sales, even in a country setting like New Hope, I think. Of course, Lydia's shop has many more practical items to highlight than our historical displays."

The conversation shifted to business matters, much to Michael's relief. Yet throughout the rest of the meal, he couldn't shake the feeling that something had created a subtle distance between them.

Anna remained warm and engaged with his family, but occasionally he caught her watching him with a guarded expression that hadn't been there during their walk. Had he hurt her somehow? The possibility bothered him more than it should have.

Their earlier conversation about what others were assuming came to mind. She'd been so sensible. What had she said? They knew what was going on between them, even if others didn't. They'd stick to that. Right?

But as Michael so belatedly had realized, he didn't know what was going on between them at all. And for sure and certain, he didn't know what she was feeling.

His supper weighed like a heavy brick in his gut. What a complete muddle he'd gotten them into.

As the evening drew to a close and the time came to escort Anna back to the Yoders', Michael found himself reluctant for their time together to end. He badly wanted to fix things between them. The day had brought a deepening appreciation for Anna—for her grace with his family as well as Samy and the Yoders, and her genuine interest in the community.

But he was at a loss for what he should say or do about any of it.

"Your family is wonderful," Anna said as they walked back along the darkening path, a lantern lighting their way. "Thank you for including me."

"They liked you very much," Michael replied honestly. "Especially my brothers. I've never seen Mason and Micah so well-behaved at supper."

Anna laughed softly. "They remind me of some of the young visitors at the museum—full of questions and boundless energy."

They walked at a comfortable pace for a while before Michael spoke again, choosing his words carefully.

"Earlier, when I mentioned the... assumptions about our relationship, I may have been too blunt. If I caused any discomfort, I apologize."

Anna was quiet for several steps before responding. "You were being honest, which I appreciate. This situation is complicated for both of us."

Her careful response revealed little of her true feelings, leaving Michael more uncertain than before and more unsure of himself.

"There's only a couple of days until the wedding," he noted, changing the subject. "Is there anything in particular you'd like to see on the island before then?"

"I've always dreamed of visiting your famous red shores and island cliffs," Anna replied. "But I'm happy to fit into whatever plans you've made."

Again, that careful politeness that kept him at a slight distance. A sudden, strong desire to break through it, to understand what she was truly thinking, pressed him to come clean with her.

"Anna," he began, slowing his pace as the Yoder farmhouse came into view in the distance. "I want you to know that I'm glad you came. Not just because of the original reason for my invitation, but because meeting you in person has been... significant."

She turned toward him, her face partially illuminated by the lantern light. "Significant?"

"Important," he clarified, struggling to find the right words. "Meaningful. I feel as though we've known each other much better than we realized. Or at least more than I realized through our correspondence. It's like I've known you for a long time, even though we've only just met face-to-face."

A small smile touched her lips. "I understand. I feel the same way."

The simple acknowledgment eased something in Michael's chest, restoring a sense of connection that had felt briefly threatened. Whatever complications lay ahead, whatever confusion their pretense might cause, he was genuinely glad to have Anna here in New Hope, in his life. In that moment, he could have hugged Samy for clicking send on his email invitation. It turned out to be the happiest accident ever.

As they approached the Yoder house, Michael's elation dimmed by wondering what would happen after the wedding, after Anna returned to Ontario. Would they simply resume their translation correspondence as if this visit had never happened? The thought left him feeling unexpectedly hollow.

Three more days. Just three days to navigate these unfamiliar feelings before life returned to normal.

Somehow, normal no longer seemed quite enough.

C hapter Eight

Samy matched her pace to Sharon's as they walked the familiar dirt path toward Noah's farm. The morning air carried the scent of wildflowers and freshly turned earth, a combination that always settled Samy's nerves. She counted her steps silently—a habit that brought comfort through its predictability.

"My *mamm* says there's a wedding coming up that everyone is talking about," Sharon said, breaking the comfortable silence between them. "Do you know them?"

Samy nodded. "*Ya*. Mark and Ellen's wedding isn't traditional Amish, though. They joined a Mennonite church, but they're still friendly with our church people." She hesitated, then added, "You could come, too, as my guest."

Sharon's eyes widened. "Really? Are you sure?"

"If your parents will allow it. My *datt* says it's a progressive church." Samy pronounced the word carefully, having heard it several times in discussions about the upcoming wedding. "But Mark and Ellen are following many of our traditions at the wedding out of respect for their Amish family."

"I'll ask my parents," Sharon said, a smile spreading across her face. "I've never been to a Mennonite church before."

They walked in silence for a few moments before Sharon asked, "Will there be boys there? From other communities?"

The question made Samy's stomach tighten slightly. At fourteen, many Amish girls began thinking about romance and courting, but the subject made Samy uncomfortable in ways she couldn't quite articulate.

"*I suppose*," she replied. "Families come from all the districts in Ontario and Pennsylvania. Some even from Ohio."

Sharon's face lit up. "That sounds exciting! Don't you think so?"

Samy shrugged. "I guess. I mostly like the food."

"But don't you want to meet someone special someday?" Sharon pressed, her voice lifting with curiosity.

Why worry over something so far away, when she had no control over the future, anyway? But before Samy could decide on an honest response that wouldn't sound stupid to her new friend, the clip-clop of hooves drew their attention. Looking up, she saw Michael's courting buggy approaching on the main road that intersected their path. Anna sat beside him, her face turned toward him in conversation.

"That's Michael Beller, our new teacher," Samy explained, pointing. "And Anna, who's staying with us. She came for Mark's wedding."

Sharon squinted against the morning sun. "They look nice together. Are they courting?"

Samy hesitated. This was exactly the type of information she wasn't supposed to share. She had promised herself she wouldn't tell anyone about the email or Michael's plan.

"Sort of," she said finally, immediately regretting her words.

Sharon noticed her discomfort. "What do you mean 'sort of'?"

"Nothing," Samy said quickly. "They only just met in person. They wrote letters before."

"About what?" Sharon's curiosity was relentless.

"Old journals. They're both good at languages." Samy tried to steer the conversation away from dangerous territory. "Anna works at a museum with her grandfather."

But Sharon wasn't easily distracted. "If they just met, why do they look so comfortable together? They're smiling like they've known each other forever."

Samy bit her lip, watching as the buggy passed by. Michael and Anna indeed looked happy together, laughing at something Samy couldn't hear. It didn't look like pretend at all.

"Maybe they like each other more than they thought they would." This must be another one of those times when what people did and what they said didn't match up. That happened far too much for Samy to figure out. She huffed. "I'm sure I don't get it at all. Maybe you can figure it out."

"Well, it seems like that would be why she came for the wedding. Because they like each other?"

The direct, if misguided, assumption made Samy's resolve crumble. "Not exactly. Michael invited her because—" She stopped herself, but it was too late.

"Because what?" Sharon prompted.

Samy sighed. She never could keep secrets well, especially when asked direct questions. "Because he wanted the matchmaking mothers to stop trying to find him a wife."

Sharon's eyes widened. "So it's fake? They're pretending?"

"It was supposed to be," Samy admitted, her voice dropping to a whisper though no one else was around to hear. "That was their agreement."

"That's so romantic," Sharon breathed. "Like a story."

Samy failed to understand what was romantic about a ridiculous deception, but that was the least of her worries now.

"You can't tell anyone," Samy said urgently. "I wasn't supposed to tell you. It was a secret."

Was.

Another sigh.

How could she be so careless?

"Don't worry." Sharon nodded solemnly. "I promise I won't tell. But," she added with a small smile, "I think everyone will figure it out soon enough. They don't look like they're pretending at all."

Samy frowned. "I think the entire business is rotten. But I really like Anna. Michael, too. And it seems like a *goot* way to both get hurt, if you ask me."

"I still think it's romantic." Sharon sighed.

As they continued walking, Samy felt the familiar weight of having said too much. No matter how hard she tried to keep secrets, the words always seemed to find their way out. It was like trying to hold water in cupped hands—the harder she tried to contain it, the faster it slipped through her fingers.

"Sharon," she said after a moment, "you really can't tell anyone. Michael is going to be our teacher, and if people think he tricked them..."

"I won't," Sharon assured her. "I'm good at keeping secrets."

Samy wished she could say the same about herself. As they approached Noah's farm, she could see the horses in the paddock and felt a rush of relief. Horses were so much simpler than people and their complicated feelings. With animals, everything was honest and clear—no pretending, no secrets, no confusion about what was real and what wasn't.

But as they entered the barn, Samy couldn't shake the image of Michael and Anna in the buggy, smiling as though they'd known each other all their lives. Was Sharon right? Had what started as pretend begun turning into something else entirely? Samy wasn't sure if that was a good thing or not.

All she knew was that secrets had a way of coming out, whether she intended them to or not.

Michael guided the horse along the winding coastal road, sneaking glances at Anna whenever he thought she wouldn't notice. The morning sun cast a golden glow across her face as she took in the island scenery with wide, appreciative eyes.

"It's beautiful here," she said, breaking a comfortable silence. "So different from Ontario."

"Prince Edward Island has its own kind of beauty," Michael agreed. "I suppose I haven't fully appreciated it for a while. Seeing it through your eyes is refreshing."

Anna nodded. "That happens with familiar places. But I don't think I could ever get tired of Prince Edward Island."

Michael doubted she had any notion of how her words made his heart skip a beat.

As they rounded a bend in the road, the vast expanse of farmland gave way to a view of Noah's horse therapy farm. Several horses grazed peacefully in the paddock, their tails swishing at flies in the morning heat.

"That's Noah Detweiler's farm," Michael explained, pointing. "It's where Samy spends most of her free time. She has a special way with the horses there."

"Samy talks of little else," Anna said, leaning forward with interest. "And her horse. Amazon?"

Michael smiled. "Amazon is Samy's favorite. OR maybe Samy is Amazon's favorite. The two have had a strong bond ever since Samy was very little. She was a foster child of *Englisch* neighbors down the road until she ran away and was found snuggled in Joel's barn with Amazon as her protectress. Later, Joel and Lydia adopted her. Then, Noah came to New Hope, married Rachel, and now runs a therapy program for children with special needs. The horses help in ways humans sometimes can't."

"That's wonderful," Anna said softly. "Samy seems to really come alive when she talks about the horses."

"She does. Noah and his wife Rachel have been a blessing to our community, especially for Samy." Michael slowed the buggy as they passed the property. "And just beyond there is the Fisher place. They're new to our community—moved in about a month ago. Their daughter Sharon has become friends with Samy, which surprised everyone. Samy doesn't usually take to new people so quickly."

"Perhaps they found common ground," Anna suggested.

"Perhaps," Michael agreed, though he still found it remarkable. "Sharon seems to have the same patience with Samy that Amazon does."

They continued along the road, the conversation flowing easily between them. Michael shared stories about growing up in New Hope that he hadn't thought about in years—the time his brother Mark had convinced him to climb the tallest maple tree on their property, only to need their father's help to get down; the winter the entire community had gathered to replace a barn roof destroyed in a snowstorm; the first day he'd successfully completed milking the entire herd by himself.

Anna listened attentively, asking questions that showed genuine interest. There was something about her that made talking come naturally, even though talking wasn't his usual inclination.

As they approached the public park that offered access to the shoreline, Michael felt an unexpected flutter of nervousness. The picnic had been his idea, a way to show Anna the island's famous red cliffs and sandy beaches, but now he worried it might seem too much like a courting move.

"Here we are," he said as he guided the horse to a hitching post near the park entrance. "The best view on this part of the island."

He helped Anna down from the buggy, momentarily aware of her hand in his and the faint scent of lavender that seemed to follow her. She smiled up at him before reaching back into the buggy for the picnic basket Lydia had prepared for them.

"Lydia insisted I take this," she said, lifting the substantial wicker basket. "She said no trip to the shore would be complete without a picnic."

"That sounds like Lydia," Michael chuckled, taking the basket from her. "Did she pack any of her fried pies? They're famous around here."

"I think so. I saw her wrapping something in waxed paper," Anna replied. "Is there a particular kind you're hoping for?"

"Cherry," Michael admitted with a small smile. "Though her apple ones are nearly as *goot*."

They found a level spot on the grassy area above the beach, with a clear view of the red cliffs and sparkling water beyond. Michael spread out the quilt Anna had brought while she began unpacking the basket.

"Cherry it is," she announced triumphantly, holding up a carefully wrapped pie. "How did she know?"

Michael felt a surprising warmth spread through his chest. "Lydia has a way of remembering everyone's favorites."

As they settled onto the quilt and began their meal, Michael became increasingly aware of how comfortable it was to be with Anna. Their conversation never felt forced or awkward, even in moments of silence.

"I should thank you again," he said after they'd finished the sandwiches and moved on to Lydia's famous pies. "For agreeing to this arrangement. It's already working exactly as I'd hoped. Mattie told me yesterday that Ada and Sarah have been redirecting their nieces' expectations."

Anna smiled, brushing a crumb from her dress. "I'm glad to help. And it's been a wonderful experience already. Your family has been so welcoming."

"They like you," Michael said simply. "You're especially easy to like."

Anna's cheeks flushed, but he wasn't sorry. He'd only spoken the truth and meant it sincerely. Still, he hurried to rectify her unease. "*Mamm* sure thinks a great deal of you already."

"She's been very kind."

"Kind isn't the word I'd use. Enthusiastic, maybe. Hopeful." Michael hesitated, then added, "I should probably warn you she's likely planning our wedding already." He chuckled, then noticed the bloom return to Anna's cheeks. He wasn't doing such a terrific job of making Anna less uncomfortable.

Anna's fingers fretted with the edge of her napkin. "Well, she'll be disappointed when I return to Ontario after the wedding."

Michael felt an unexpected pang at her words. "Actually, I was wondering about that. Do you need to leave right after the wedding? Maybe you could stay a little longer."

Anna looked surprised at his question. "I thought you knew. I'll be here through next weekend at least."

Michael blinked. "I didn't realize you'd be staying so long."

"How else would we have time to work on the translation?" Anna asked practically. "I brought the journal copies with me. I thought that was part of why you invited me."

"Of course," Michael said quickly, though in truth he hadn't thought that far ahead when he'd written the email to her. "That makes perfect sense."

Michael looked out over the water, quietly pleased.

"Is that a problem?" Anna asked, noticing his thoughtful expression.

"Not at all," he assured her, turning back with a smile. "I'm glad you'll be staying longer. There's so much more of the island to show you. And the translation work, of course."

She studied him for a moment, as if trying to read something in his expression. "Of course," she agreed softly.

Michael took another bite of his cherry pie, savoring the sweet-tart flavor. The sun warmed his face, and the waves provided a gentle soundtrack, and beside him sat a woman who understood his passion for old languages and forgotten stories. For a moment, he allowed himself to forget that their time together was destined to end, when Anna would eventually return to her life in Ontario, and that he had responsibilities to the community that had entrusted him with their children's education.

For now, it was enough to sit beside her on a red beach under a blue sky, sharing cherry pies and conversation that felt as natural as breathing.

Anna leaned back on her hands, her legs stretched out before her on the quilt. The sound of waves breaking against the shore created a peaceful backdrop to their conversation. She watched Michael as he described the summer festivals the island hosted each year, his hands animated as he spoke about the music and community gatherings.

"The island's strawberry festivals are my favorite," he admitted, his eyes bright with enthusiasm. "The entire community comes together. Even though we observe differently than our *Englisch* neighbors, we've found ways to participate that honor our traditions."

"I didn't realize there was so much interaction between communities," Anna said, genuinely curious.

Michael smiled. "Our settlement here is a bit more... flexible than some others. Bishop Nafzinger believes socializing with others in the community helps us be better neighbors. We don't participate in everything, of course, but we aren't hiding our light under a bushel, so to speak."

"I like that." She smiled. "What should I expect at Mark and Ellen's wedding. I've never attended an Amish wedding before, although I understand theirs will be a mix of Amish and what is probably more familiar to me."

"The church service itself will be more like what you are used to with their own pastor officiating," Michael explained. "Afterward, things will follow more along our traditions. There'll be a large luncheon for all the guests, activities all afternoon, the wedding supper where so many will partner up with a date, and a hymn sing for the youngies in the evening."

Anna nodded, taking in the information. "Will we sit together during the luncheon?"

"Actually, no," Michael replied. "I'll be seated with Mark and the immediate family. It's tradition." He must have noticed her expression fall slightly, because he quickly added, "But we'll be seated together at the evening meal. And I'll be sure to keep you company during the day."

"I see," Anna said, trying not to sound disappointed. The thought of navigating a room full of strangers without Michael by her side was more daunting than she wanted to admit.

"After the meal, there will be games—softball, volleyball, that sort of thing. The younger people especially enjoy that part," Michael continued. "Then the evening meal, and afterward, singing that often goes late into the night."

Anna tried to imagine Michael singing—his deep voice joining with others in hymns, perhaps even smiling in a way she hadn't yet seen. The image warmed her unexpectedly.

"I've never been much of a singer," she confessed. "My friends always tease me about being tone deaf."

"I don't believe that," Michael replied, his voice gentler than before. "Perhaps you just haven't found the right harmony yet. I am very glad you'll be with me, Anna. There's no one I'd rather share the day with than you."

The comment hung between them, weighted with potential meaning. Anna felt her cheeks warm and looked away toward the sea, where the afternoon sun sparkled on the water like scattered diamonds.

"Tell me about your family," Michael said after a moment. "You've met mine now, but I know so little about yours beyond your grandfather."

Anna gathered her thoughts, smoothing a wrinkle in her skirt. "There's not much to tell, really. It's just *Dawdi* and me now. My parents..." she hesitated, the familiar tightness forming in her chest. "My mother left when I was three. She wasn't raised Mennonite, and I think she found our lifestyle too restrictive. She and my dad divorced and left me with his parents to raise, but my grandmother had a weak heart. Soon it was just the two of us, me and *Dawdi*."

Michael's expression softened with sympathy. "I'm sorry."

"It was a long time ago," Anna said with a practiced casualness she didn't entirely feel. "My father died when I was twelve—in a farming accident. But he'd never really taken much interest in my life after the divorce."

"That must have been difficult."

Anna nodded. "It was. But *Dawdi* needed me as much as I did him. The museum became our shared purpose. All those artifacts and journals—each one tells a story of someone who faced their own struggles and persevered. It helped somehow to read their stories."

"Is that why you're so interested in translation work?" Michael asked. "To preserve their stories and give voice to people from the past?"

Anna looked at him with surprise. No one had ever made that connection before.

"I suppose it is," she almost whispered. "I never thought of it quite that way."

They sat in comfortable silence for a moment, watching a pair of gulls circle above the water. Anna was struck by how easily Michael seemed to understand her motivations, even ones she hadn't fully recognized herself.

"What about your future?" Michael asked. "Do you plan to continue working at the museum indefinitely?"

"*Dawdi* is supportive, though I think he hopes I'll eventually take over the museum completely," Anna admitted.

"And is that what you want?"

The directness of his question caught her off guard. "I'm not entirely sure," she said honestly. "I love the work, but sometimes I wonder... Well, I don't know how to put it that doesn't sound terribly ungrateful. But I wonder what it would be like to have a family and purpose beyond the museum."

Michael nodded thoughtfully. "I understand that feeling. My family have all been farmers for generations, but learning fulfills me in a way that farming never could."

"Is that why you accepted the offer to become a teacher?" Anna asked, genuinely curious about this man, who seemed to defy the expectations of his community in subtle ways.

"Partly," Michael replied. "I've always loved learning. As a boy, I would read anything I could get my hands on—much to my father's concern sometimes." He smiled at the memory. "But watching my sister teach these past several years, I believed I could make a difference in our community if I accepted their offer to teach. The children are our future, after all."

A smile tipped up the corners of her mouth. There was something admirable about his dedication, his willingness to forge a path that balanced tradition with his own calling.

"What?" he asked, noticing her expression.

"Nothing," she replied. "I just... I think you'll be an excellent teacher."

Their eyes met, and for a moment, Anna felt something shift between them—a current of understanding that went beyond their translation connection or their pretend courtship. Michael's gaze dropped briefly to her lips, then returned to her eyes, a question forming there that made her breath catch.

He leaned forward slightly, and Anna did the same, drawn by something she couldn't quite name.

"Michael Beller! Is that you?"

The moment shattered as a cheerful voice called from the beach below. Anna and Michael both startled, pulling back as they turned toward the sound.

A young man and woman were making their way up from the shore, hand in hand. The man waved enthusiastically, his broad smile visible even from a distance.

"Drew," Michael murmured, the name sounding like both recognition and mild disappointment. He stood, brushing sand from his trousers, and raised a hand in greeting.

Anna stood as well, smoothing her dress and hoping the flush she felt in her cheeks wasn't as visible as it seemed.

"Michael! I thought that was you," the young man said as he approached, his companion smiling shyly beside him. "We just arrived from Ontario yesterday for the wedding."

"Drew Erb," Michael said, shaking the man's hand firmly. "It's good to see you. And Emma too," he added, nodding politely to the young woman.

"It's been too long," Drew agreed, his gaze shifting curiously to Anna.

"This is Anna Roth," Michael said, placing a hand lightly at the small of her back in a touch of gentle protectiveness. "She'll be attending the wedding as well."

"Anna," Drew repeated. "It's a pleasure to meet you."

"Likewise," Anna replied, trying to quell the lingering sensation from the almost-moment with Michael.

"Are you from the island?" Emma asked in a soft voice.

"No, Ontario," Anna explained. "I work with my grandfather at his museum there."

Drew's eyes widened with recognition. "The Mennonite Heritage Museum? I've visited there with my family."

"That's the one," Anna confirmed with a smile.

"So you and Michael are..." Drew let the question hang, glancing between them with undisguised curiosity.

"Friends," Michael supplied smoothly. "Anna and I have been corresponding about a translation project."

Anna felt a twinge of something—disappointment, perhaps—at his description, though it was entirely accurate.

"How nice," Emma said, though her expression suggested she suspected there was more to the story.

"I assume you'll be at the wedding?" Emma added, turning to Anna. "Will you know many people there?"

"Just the Yoders, whom I'm staying with, and Michael's family," Anna admitted.

Emma's face brightened. "Well, now you know us too! You must sit with Drew and me for lunch while Michael is stuck with the wedding party."

Anna felt a wave of relief wash over her. "I'd like that very much. Thank you."

"It's settled then," Emma said with a warm smile. "I'll look for you after the ceremony. Don't worry—I won't let you get lost in the crowd."

"We should let you return to your picnic," Drew said, his eyes twinkling with amusement.

After a few more pleasantries, Drew and Emma continued their walk along the shoreline, occasionally glancing back with knowing smiles that made Anna feel oddly exposed.

"Drew was in school with me," Michael explained as they watched the couple depart. "He's Lydia's nephew. His *datt* is her brother. One of them. She has another brother that lives in a different community."

"Ah," Anna said, understanding dawning. "So, he probably already knew about us... I mean me. News travels quickly, I'm sure."

"I'm afraid so," Michael agreed, turning back to her with an apologetic smile. "Does that bother you?"

Anna considered the question honestly. "No," she finally said. "That was the purpose of this arrangement, wasn't it? To give the impression that you're not... available for matchmaking?"

"It was," Michael confirmed, though something in his expression had changed. "But I didn't imagine us being seen together like this."

Michael studied her face for a moment, as if searching for something.

"I don't mind," Anna said, surprised to find she meant it. "I'm not embarrassed, if that what you mean. Your family has been lovely, and I'm enjoying my time here more than I expected. And now I've met Emma, which is a relief. I was worried about not knowing anyone at the wedding while you're with your family."

"I'm glad," he said simply. "Emma is kind. You'll be in *goot* hands."

As they began packing up their picnic, Anna's thoughts replayed that brief moment before Drew's interruption. What had almost happened? And why did she feel so disappointed that it hadn't?

"We should probably head back," Michael said, folding the quilt carefully. "Samy will be returning from Noah's farm soon, and she gets anxious if her routine is disrupted."

"Of course," Anna agreed, helping him gather the remaining items.

As they walked back to the buggy, side by side but no longer quite touching, Anna tried to remind herself of the practical realities of their situation.

She was Mennonite. He was Amish. She had a life and responsibilities in Ontario. He had his here on the island. Their arrangement was temporary—a convenient solution to a specific problem.

Yet as Michael helped her into the buggy, his hand warm and strong around hers, Anna couldn't deny the growing feeling that what had begun as pretense was becoming something else entirely. Something real, complicated, and potentially heartbreaking.

She just wasn't sure what to do about it.

C hapter Nine

Michael hefted another bench from the wagon, carrying it toward the barn where Mark and Ellen's wedding reception would be held the following day. The Beller farm had been transformed—additional tables borrowed from neighboring families, benches arranged in neat rows, and the barn swept clean until it gleamed.

"Careful with that one," his father called from across the yard. "It's got a wobbly side that needs fixed. I already told Myles to take care of it."

Michael nodded, setting the bench in its designated spot. Around him, the controlled chaos of wedding preparation continued. His brothers moved with practiced efficiency, having helped with numerous community weddings over the years.

At least for Mark and Ellen's there was no need to set up the barn for church, since their wedding ceremony would take place in the Mennonite church building. But the rest of the day was to be set up exactly as they had done on the farm for his sister's wedding. And as he supposed they would one day do for his own.

His thoughts drifted to the moment when his lips had almost touched Anna's the day before. The smell of saltwater and the cool ocean breeze might well have still been tickling his senses as he remembered the sweetness of being so close to her.

What would have happened if Drew hadn't interrupted? He was fairly certain she would have allowed him to kiss her. She leaned toward him as much as he had to her. He was sure she had. But then what? Where would he take things from there? He couldn't leave New Hope. Not now.

And he wasn't like Mark. He was Amish through and through. And Anna was Mennonite. He wouldn't ask her to change for him. As much as he wished Drew had walked a different path with Emma, perhaps it was for the best he came along when he did.

The sound of buggy wheels on gravel drew his attention. Another group of wedding guests had arrived from Ontario, their travel-weary faces brightening as they spotted familiar community members. Michael watched as his mother emerged from the house to greet them, her arms already extended in welcome.

Among the arrivals, he spotted two young women who could only be Leah and Heather—the matchmaking targets Ada and Sarah had been discussing for weeks. Both appeared to be in their early twenties, dressed in the modest attire of their respective communities. Leah, the taller of the two, had dark hair beneath her head covering and moved with quiet confidence. Heather was shorter, with light brown hair and an animated expression as she spoke with the other travelers.

Michael felt a twist of guilt watching them. These women had traveled considerable distances partly because they'd been told about an unmarried Amish schoolteacher. Now they would discover he was supposedly courting someone else—a deception that felt increasingly uncomfortable. Only for an altogether different reason than at the start, because now he wished it were true when it couldn't be.

"The matchmaking prospects have arrived," Myles observed, appearing at Michael's side with another bench. "Ada and Sarah will be pleased."

"They'll be disappointed soon enough," Michael replied, more sharply than he'd intended.

Myles raised an eyebrow. "Because of Anna?"

The simple question carried layers of implication. Because of their pretense? Because of Michael's growing genuine feelings? Because of the religious barriers between them? Michael wasn't sure how to answer.

"It's complicated," he said finally.

"Most worthwhile things are," Myles replied with unexpected wisdom for his eighteen years. "But Anna seems to fit here. With us, I mean. With you."

Before Michael could respond, his mother's voice carried across the yard. "Michael! Come meet our guests!"

He straightened his shoulders, preparing for what would likely be an awkward introduction. As he approached the group, Belinda's expression held the neutral politeness she used when navigating delicate social situations.

"Michael, I'd like you to meet Leah Erb and Heather Gingerich," she said, gesturing to the two young women. "They've traveled from Ontario for the wedding."

"Welcome to Prince Edward Island," Michael said, extending his hand to each in turn. "I hope your journey wasn't too difficult."

"Not at all," Leah replied, her voice soft but clear. "We're grateful to be here for such a joyous occasion."

"Indeed," Heather added, her eyes sparkling with obvious excitement. "We've heard so much about the island community. Everyone speaks of how close-knit and welcoming it is."

Michael nodded, acutely aware of Ada and Sarah watching the interaction from nearby. Their expressions held a mixture of hope and calculation that made him increasingly uncomfortable.

"You'll find plenty of opportunities to experience that hospitality over the next few days," he replied diplomatically.

"Michael teaches at our school," Ada interjected, moving closer to the group. "He'll be starting his first term this fall."

"How wonderful," Leah said with genuine interest. "Teaching is such important work. Do you enjoy it?"

"I'm looking forward to it," Michael answered honestly. "Though I haven't officially started yet."

"Leah has experience helping with Sunday school in her district," Sarah added pointedly. "She has quite a way with children."

The transparent attempt at matchmaking made Michael's jaw tighten slightly. "That's admirable," he managed.

An uncomfortable silence fell over the group before Heather spoke up. "We understand there will be games and activities after tomorrow's ceremony. It sounds like great fun."

"There will be," Michael confirmed. "Volleyball, softball, that sort of thing. The younger people especially enjoy that part of the celebration."

"Perhaps you could help organize some of the activities?" Ada suggested, her tone carefully casual. "Michael, you and the other young men could arrange teams..."

"Actually," Michael interrupted, seizing an opportunity to redirect the conversation, "I should mention that I've invited a guest for the wedding as well. Anna Roth, from Ontario. She's staying with the Yoders."

The announcement had the desired effect of deflating Ada and Sarah's enthusiasm, though both women maintained their polite expressions. They had known already, of course. But he winced at the surprise on the faces of the two young women. Apparently, they hadn't been told yet.

"*Ach*, Mattie did mention that just the other day. So, she has come after all, then?" Sarah said, not waiting for a response. "How nice to have more *youngies* visiting. Which district in Ontario is she from again?"

"She's Mennonite," Michael replied, understanding the intent to disqualify Anna as a serious courting option for him. "We've been corresponding for a long time—" He abruptly decided not to mention the actual nature of their letters.

Leah and Heather exchanged a glance that Michael couldn't quite interpret. Understanding? Disappointment? Relief?

"How interesting," Leah said diplomatically. "It must be wonderful to see each other in person, then."

Her gracious response impressed Michael. Despite the obvious awkwardness of the situation, she showed no signs of wounded pride or resentment.

"We look forward to meeting her," Heather added with what seemed like genuine warmth.

The generous spirit both women displayed made Michael feel even worse about the deception. They deserved better than to be unwitting participants in his charade.

"I should get back to work," he said, excusing himself from the group. "We still have several loads of benches to unload."

As he walked away, Michael caught fragments of conversation behind him—Ada and Sarah's disappointed murmurs, his mother's diplomatic responses, and the young guests' uninterrupted excitement to be there.

Tomorrow, Anna would meet these women in person. Leah and Heather both seemed kind, and neither appeared disappointed like their older relatives. And then, the thought of Anna having to navigate questions about their relationship made him feel protective in a way that surprised him with its intensity.

He ought to have been more honest about their correspondence. Why hadn't he? His conscience warred within.

"Everything all right?" Mark appeared beside him, carrying another bench. "You look like a man with something weighing on his mind."

Michael glanced at his older brother—the groom, who would tomorrow pledge his life to Ellen despite the complications that Mark's leaving the Amish had initially created. If anyone understood complex romantic situations, it would be Mark.

"Just thinking about tomorrow," Michael replied carefully.

"Nervous about introducing Anna to more of the community?" Mark's knowing smile suggested he saw through Michael's evasive answer.

"Something like that."

Mark set down his bench and studied Michael's face. "You know, when I first met Ellen, I knew she was the one for me. But then, all I saw were the obstacles, and my choices complicated things even more."

"But you worked it out," Michael observed. "Took six years, though."

"I'm a slow learner, but maybe you can learn from my mistakes," Mark laughed, then turned serious. "The question isn't whether there are obstacles—there always are. The question is whether what you've found is worth overcoming them."

The advice hung in the air as Mark picked up his bench and continued toward the barn. Michael stood alone in the yard, watching the continued preparations around him while wrestling with his brother's words.

Worth overcoming the obstacles. But what exactly had he found with Anna? A genuine connection that went beyond their translation collaboration? Or was his own loneliness causing him to mistake Anna's gentle company for something deeper on her part?

Tomorrow would likely provide some answers, whether he was ready for them or not. As the afternoon wore on and more guests arrived, Michael watched for Anna's return from her afternoon at Noah's farm with Samy. He had promised to escort her to the evening meal at Mattie and Winston's house with both his family and bride's too. There'd be even more people who would assume their relationship was genuine.

He wasn't sure he would have to pretend anymore, at least for his part. But what about hers? The thought of Anna leaving after the wedding—returning to her quiet life in Ontario while he remained here—left him feeling unexpectedly hollow.

Perhaps Mark was right. Perhaps the question wasn't whether there were complications, but whether what he'd discovered with Anna was worth fighting for, despite the apparent impossibility of it all.

Despite not knowing if she even wanted him to fight for her.

Anna carefully arranged wildflowers in mason jars, creating simple centerpieces for the wedding tables. The Yoder kitchen had been transformed into a bustling hub of activity, with women from the community working together to prepare food and decorations for tomorrow's celebration.

"These are lovely, Anna," Lydia said, pausing to admire the arrangements. "You have an artistic eye."

"Thank you," Anna replied, adjusting a spray of Queen Anne's lace. "We do similar displays at the museum for special events."

The familiar work was soothing, even amid the controlled chaos around her. Anna had quickly fallen into the rhythm of the preparation activities, finding comfort in the shared purpose and easy camaraderie among the women.

"Anna," Lydia called from across the kitchen, "I'd like you to meet some of our visiting guests. Leah Erb and Heather Gingerich have just arrived from Ontario."

Anna looked up to see two young women approaching, both dressed in the modest attire of their respective communities. The taller one, with dark hair beneath her prayer covering, moved with quiet grace. The shorter one had light brown hair and an open, friendly expression.

"Anna Roth," she said, extending her hand with a welcoming smile. "It's so nice to meet you both."

"Leah Erb," the taller woman replied, her handshake firm and warm. "We've heard you're visiting from Ontario as well. Which community are you from?"

"Near Kitchener," Anna answered. "My grandfather and I run a small Mennonite heritage museum there."

"How fascinating," Heather said with genuine interest. "I'm Heather Gingerich, by the way. What kind of exhibits do you have?"

Anna found herself immediately drawn into a conversation about the museum's collections and the joy of connecting visitors with their heritage. Both women listened with genuine interest and thoughtful questions. She found them not so different from her friends back home.

"You must find your work very fulfilling," Leah observed. "Preserving stories from the past for future generations—that's important work."

"I do," Anna agreed. "Though sometimes I wonder if there's more I could be doing to reach people, to make history come alive for them."

"Perhaps through teaching?" Heather suggested. "You could share your expertise in schools as a guest."

The suggestion sparked an unexpected flutter of interest in Anna's chest. She'd never seriously considered teaching in a school, but the idea of sharing her passion for history in a school setting appealed to her greatly.

"That's an interesting thought," she mused. "Perhaps there could be opportunities to speak at our schools."

"Anna has been helping Michael with translation work," Lydia interjected as she passed by with a tray of freshly baked bread. "Old journals in several European languages."

Anna noticed both women's expressions shift slightly at the mention of Michael's name, though they maintained their polite smiles.

"I think that's wonderful," Leah said diplomatically. "Michael seems like a very thoughtful young man. We met him briefly this afternoon."

Heather added, "It must be nice to have someone who shares your interests."

There was something in their tone—not unfriendly, but carefully neutral—that made Anna wonder what they'd been told about Michael before arriving. Had they come here with expectations regarding him? The thought made her uncomfortable, reminding her of the deception she and Michael were maintaining.

"Yes, it's been very helpful to have his expertise with the more difficult passages," Anna replied honestly. "His knowledge has advanced our work considerably."

Ada Gingerich appeared at Heather's shoulder, her expression bright with forced cheer. "Anna, how lovely to finally meet you. We've heard so much about your visit."

"All good things, I hope," Anna replied with a smile, though something in Ada's tone put her on guard.

"Oh, absolutely," Ada assured her, though her eyes held a calculating quality. "It's wonderful that you and Michael can work together on our shared heritage. Though I'm sure there must be challenges, with your communities being so different."

The comment was delivered with a sweet smile, but Anna caught the subtle probing beneath it. Ada was searching for information about her relationship with Michael, perhaps hoping to find cracks in what she assumed was a romantic attachment.

"Different communities often have much in common," Anna replied carefully. "Shared values, similar traditions. The differences can be quite minor when you focus on what unites rather than what divides."

Leah's expression warmed at Anna's response. "That's a lovely way to look at it."

"Indeed," Heather agreed. "Faith communities should support one another, shouldn't they?"

Anna found herself genuinely liking both women. Their gracious acceptance of what they presumably saw as disappointing news—that Michael was unavailable—spoke well of their character. They seemed more interested in genuine friendship than in competing for his attention.

"Have either of you been to Prince Edward Island before?" Anna asked, seeking to redirect the conversation to safer ground.

"I grew up here, but my family moved to another community on the island some years ago." Leah replied.

"This is my first time here," Heather chimed in. "Though the journey was long, it's been worth it just to see this place. The island is even more beautiful than I'd imagined. The red soil and ocean views are quite striking. And the wedding preparations are so exciting—I love how the whole community comes together for celebrations like this."

As the afternoon progressed, Anna worked alongside both women, preparing vegetables for tomorrow's feast and arranging flowers. Their straightforward conversation and willingness to pitch in wherever needed impressed her. Whatever disappointment they might have felt about Michael's situation, they showed no signs of resentment or awkwardness.

"Anna," Sarah Erb approached the group, her expression holding the same forced brightness as Ada's had earlier. "I understand you'll be sitting with Michael at tomorrow's evening meal?"

The question was clearly intended to confirm the romantic nature of their relationship. Anna felt heat rise in her cheeks, aware that Leah and Heather were listening carefully to her response.

"Yes," she replied simply, not trusting herself to elaborate without revealing her discomfort with the deception.

"Well then," Sarah continued, "I'm sure you're both very happy."

The assumption made Anna's stomach twist with guilt. "We're very comfortable together," Anna said finally, choosing words that were technically true while avoiding outright lies.

Leah gave her a gentle smile that suggested understanding. "Comfort and shared interests are wonderful foundations," she said quietly. "My *Aenti*

Rachel often reminds me that friendship is the best beginning for deeper relationships."

The kindness in her voice only increased Anna's guilt. Here was a woman who had presumably been interested in Michael, only to discover he was unavailable. Yet instead of resentment, she offered gracious words of support.

"Thank you," Anna replied, her voice softer than she'd intended. "That's very wise advice. Do you mean that Rachel Detweiler is your aunt?" Anna thought of Noah's wife, whom she'd met at their horse therapy farm, and thought she could see a family resemblance.

A soft smile curved Leah's lips at the mention of Rachel's name. "She is my *datt's* sister, as well as Sarah. But Rachel is the youngest, like me. I don't get to see her often, but I do love her so. Our families have drifted apart since..." Her voice trailed off as her aunt Sarah passed by and the topic was dropped.

Anna didn't want to pry. But she got a sense that Leah would very much like to be a part of New Hope rather than wherever her father had moved her family. Again, a twinge of guilt nagged at her conscience.

As the sun began to set and the preparation activities wound down, Anna helped to clean up alongside Leah and Heather. The three women worked in comfortable silence, and Anna realized how much she would have enjoyed their friendship under different circumstances.

"We should probably head to our lodgings," Heather said as they finished drying the last of the serving dishes. "Tomorrow will be a long, wonderful day."

"I'm sure I'll see you both tomorrow," Anna said. "I can introduce you to Emma. And perhaps we could sit together during some of the afternoon activities?"

"We'd like that very much," Heather agreed warmly. "It will be nice to have more friends at the celebration."

After the women departed, Anna helped Lydia finish the final preparations in the kitchen. As they worked, she thought about the afternoon's interactions.

"Leah and Heather seem like lovely women," she commented.

"They are," Lydia agreed. "It's a shame they were drawn here on somewhat false pretenses, only to discover Michael was already spoken for. Though they've taken the news graciously."

Anna's hands stilled on the dish she was drying. "I'm sorry."

Lydia glanced at her with surprise. "Oh, dear. You aren't to blame. Ada and Sarah have been planning for weeks to introduce Michael to suitable young women. Leah and Heather were their top candidates. But it seems *Gott's* plans were different."

"I...," Anna struggled to find the words to explain what was really happening. Only she wasn't sure herself. After all, it did appear that God's plans for this trip may indeed be very different than she had thought.

"Well, it all worked out for the best, didn't it?" Lydia said with a warm smile. "Michael found someone who truly suits him before Ada and Sarah could complicate matters with their matchmaking schemes."

Anna nodded mutely, unable to trust her voice. The weight of the deception felt suddenly unbearable.

What had begun as a simple favor was becoming something much more complicated—not just because of her growing feelings for Michael, but because of the real consequences their pretense was having on others.

As she prepared for bed that night, Anna wondered if honesty might be kinder than their well-intentioned deception. But it was too late for such realizations now. Tomorrow was the wedding, and she would have to see their charade through to its conclusion—a conclusion that.

C hapter Ten

Anna woke before dawn on Mark and Ellen's wedding day to the sound of quiet activity throughout the Yoder household. The pre-dawn darkness was already filled with the purposeful movements of a family preparing for one of the most significant celebrations on their community calendar.

Beside her, Samy's bed was empty, the covers pulled neat and tight. Anna could hear voices downstairs—Lydia coordinating final food preparations, Joel organizing transportation, and the excited chatter of Owen and Paul discussing the day's anticipated festivities.

Anna dressed carefully in her finest dress—a deep navy blue her grandfather had agreed was "appropriate for such an important occasion." As she arranged her prayer covering over her carefully pinned hair, she caught her reflection in the small mirror above the dresser. Her face looked composed, but her eyes betrayed the nervous anticipation churning in her stomach.

Today, she would officially sit beside Michael as his companion at the evening meal. They'd be on full display before the entire community, including Leah and Heather. The thought made her stomach tighten with guilt and something else she didn't want to examine too closely—a flutter of longing for their charade to be real.

Downstairs, the kitchen was alive with controlled chaos. Lydia stood at the stove, stirring a large pot of what smelled like wedding soup, while several neighboring women arranged covered dishes on the counter. The dining table had been pushed against the wall to make room for the constant flow of helpers carrying food to wagons outside.

"Good morning, Anna," Lydia called warmly. "Perfect timing—could you help carry these pies? We're taking as much as we can down to the Beller place early."

Anna gladly accepted the task, grateful for something concrete to do with her nervous energy. As she carefully carried the pies outside, she spotted Michael across the yard helping to load the goods. Their eyes met briefly, and he offered a small smile that made her heart skip in a way that had nothing to do with their pretense.

"Anna!" Samy appeared at her elbow, practically bouncing with excitement. "Sharon is coming to the wedding. Her whole family is coming to the Bellers afterwards, too."

The girl's enthusiasm was infectious, and Anna smiled despite her nervousness. "That's wonderful, Samy. You'll have friends to enjoy the celebration with."

"You will too," Samy said with characteristic directness. "You have Michael. Everyone's talking about it."

Anna's cheeks warmed. "Are they?"

Samy paused, studying Anna's face with her unnervingly perceptive gaze. "You look nervous."

"A little," Anna admitted. "It's a big day."

"For Mark and Ellen," Samy agreed. "But also for you and Michael. Everyone will be watching to see how you act together."

The blunt observation made Anna's nervousness spike. "Watching for what?"

"To see if your wedding will be next." Samy's matter-of-fact tone made Anna's heart race. "Of course they don't know you're pretending. But don't worry. Sharon thinks you look like you're in love for real, so probably other people will think so too."

Before Anna could respond to this startling revelation, Samy bounded away to help with another task, leaving Anna standing frozen beside the wagon with a pie in her hands.

Did she and Michael really look like they were in love? The thought was both thrilling and terrifying. If their feelings were that obvious to a fourteen-year-old friend of Samy's, what would the rest of the community see when they watched them together today?

"Anna?" Belinda Beller appeared beside her, concern in her voice. "Are you alright? You look a bit pale."

"Oh, yes," Anna replied quickly, realizing she'd been standing motionless for too long. "Just thinking about the day ahead."

Belinda's expression softened with understanding. "Wedding days can be overwhelming, but don't worry—you'll do beautifully. Michael is fortunate to have found someone who fits so naturally into our community."

The kind words only intensified Anna's guilt. If Belinda only knew the truth about their arrangement...

"Thank you," Anna managed. "Your family has been incredibly welcoming."

"Because we can see how happy Michael is," Belinda replied with a warm smile. "That's all any mother wants for her children—to find someone who brings out the best in them."

As Belinda moved away to coordinate other preparations, Anna set the pie carefully in the wagon and tried to compose herself. The weight of everyone's expectations—their assumptions about her relationship with Michael—felt heavier with each passing moment.

The morning flew by in a blur of final preparations. Anna found herself swept into the stream of women heading to the Mennonite church where the ceremony would take place. The building was modest but lovely, with simple wooden pews and clear glass windows that let in the morning light.

Anna slipped into a pew with the Yoder family, noting how everyone naturally organized themselves—Amish families together, Mennonite families nearby, all united in their celebration of Mark and Ellen's union. She spotted Leah and Heather several rows ahead, sitting with what appeared to be a large extended family group.

As the ceremony began with the traditional hymns, Anna found herself moved by the simple beauty of the service. Ellen looked radiant in her modest blue dress, her face glowing with happiness as she stood beside Mark. The vows they exchanged were heartfelt and sincere, speaking of commitment, faith and the joining of two lives into one.

During the long service, Anna occasionally caught Michael making eye contact with her. The connection she felt in those moments seemed to transcend their complicated situation.

When the ceremony concluded and the congregation moved outside for congratulations and fellowship, Anna was swept into the celebration. The joy was infectious—children running between groups of adults, elderly relatives sharing stories, young people eager for the afternoon's activities.

"Anna!" Emma appeared at her side, Drew close behind. "Wasn't that beautiful? Ellen looked so happy."

"It was lovely," Anna agreed sincerely. "Such a meaningful ceremony."

"Drew was telling me about the games planned for this afternoon," Emma continued. "Volleyball, softball, some relay races. It should be great fun."

"I'm looking forward to it," Anna replied, though her attention was partially focused on scanning the crowd for Michael. She spotted him near the church entrance, accepting congratulations from community members and looking handsomer than ever in his best suit.

"There's Michael," Drew observed, following her gaze. "Should we go congratulate the brother of the groom?"

As they made their way through the crowd, Anna noticed Leah and Heather standing nearby with their host family. Both women looked lovely in their best dresses, and Anna was surprised to observe that neither were watching Michael with any particular longing or disappointment. Instead, Leah appeared to be engaged in animated conversation with a young man Anna didn't recognize, while Heather was laughing at something one of the Miller cousins had said.

Perhaps their gracious acceptance of Michael's unavailability was more genuine than Anna had assumed. The observation eased some of her guilt, though it also raised new questions about her own feelings and motivations.

"Anna," Michael greeted her with a warm smile as their group approached. "How did you find the ceremony?"

"Beautiful," she replied honestly. "Your brother and Ellen are clearly very happy together."

"They are," Michael agreed, his expression softening as he glanced toward where Mark and Ellen were receiving congratulations. "It's been a long journey for them, but they've found their way."

The comment seemed to carry additional meaning, and Anna wondered if he was thinking about their own complicated situation. Before she could analyze it further, the crowd began moving toward the buggies and hired driver services that would transport everyone to the Beller farm for the luncheon.

"Shall we?" Michael offered his arm with formal politeness, though the gesture sent warmth through Anna's chest.

As they walked toward the transportation, Anna caught sight of Leah speaking earnestly with the same young man from earlier. The man's attention was completely focused on Leah, and her animated gestures suggested she was equally engaged in their conversation.

"Who is the man speaking to Leah?" she asked Michael. "I don't think I've met him."

"I believe he is related to Noah's new neighbors. He's considering moving to New Hope as well.

Mark invited him... Joe Peters, I think that's what Mark told me."

"I see. I'm glad she's found someone she seems so pleased to talk to."

Michael gave her a meaningful look. "It's a blessing for sure to be with someone who is easy to talk to." He squeezed her hand that was resting on his arm.

"Indeed, it is." Anna swallowed at the lump of emotion forming in her chest.

Maybe, Anna thought with growing hope, this day wouldn't be as difficult as she'd feared. Perhaps everyone would find their own happiness, even if it wasn't what had originally been planned.

The thought gave her the courage to smile genuinely at Michael as he helped her into a two-seater buggy—a courting buggy, no less.

"Ready for the rest of the celebration?" she asked as he climbed in beside her and took the reins.

"With you beside me?" he replied quietly, his voice carrying a note that made her heart race. "I'm ready for anything."

Michael straightened his shirt one more time, checking his reflection in the small mirror hanging in his parents' bedroom. The morning had passed in a blur of ceremony and congratulations. But now came the part he'd long dreaded—the community celebration where he and Anna would be observed together as a couple.

Only his feeling was far from dread. Instead, he was eager to have Anna by his side throughout the rest of the day. The anxiousness he felt now was of a completely different sort.

Through the window, he could see the organized chaos of the wedding luncheon in full swing. Tables bowed under the weight of traditional wedding foods, children darted between groups of adults, and the sound of conversation and laughter filled the air. It was exactly the kind of joyous community gathering that made him grateful to be part of New Hope's close-knit district.

But today, he would navigate it all while precariously balancing a relationship that felt increasingly complicated.

A knock on the door interrupted his thoughts. "Come in."

Mark entered, still glowing with the happiness of a newly married man. "Hiding out?" he asked with an amused smile.

"Just gathering my thoughts," Michael replied, smoothing his hair one more time.

"About Anna?"

The direct question caught Michael off guard. "Mostly. *Ya*."

Mark closed the door behind him and leaned against it, studying his brother's face. "You know, watching you two during the ceremony was interesting."

"Oh?" Michael tried to keep his tone neutral. "I would have thought you only had eyes for your bride."

"True enough. But I didn't miss the way you kept looking for her in the crowd, or your expression when you spotted her—it reminded me of something."

"What?"

"How I felt the first time I realized I was falling in love with Ellen." Mark's knowing smile made Michael's stomach tighten. "The difference was, I wasn't fighting it. Not in the beginning, at least. But you seem determined to maintain some kind of distance."

Michael turned back to the mirror, unable to meet his brother's perceptive gaze. "It's complicated."

"The best things usually are," Mark replied. "But running from your feelings won't make them go away. Trust me, I tried that approach."

"This situation is different than yours was."

"Is it?" Mark moved to stand beside him, both brothers visible in the small mirror. "You've found someone who challenges you intellectually, fits into our family, brings out qualities in you we didn't even know were there. Seems similar enough to me."

Michael sighed. "Anna is Mennonite. I'm Amish. Even if there were genuine feelings between us—which I'm not saying there are—one of us would have to leave our community."

"Ellen was Amish too," Mark pointed out. "And I had left the community altogether."

"But you came back," Michael said quietly. "And compromised by joining a Mennonite church. I don't think I could do that. I belong here. And Anna..."

"I found where I belonged," Mark corrected. "It wasn't about leaving something behind—it was about moving toward something better. Do you know how Anna feels about it?"

Before Michael could respond, voices outside indicated the luncheon was ready to begin. He and Mark needed to get back to their place with the wedding party.

Mark clapped a hand on his shoulder. "All I'm saying is don't be so quick to assume the obstacles are insurmountable. Sometimes, the thing we think is impossible is exactly what we need." He headed toward the door, then paused. "Besides, from what I observed, Anna doesn't look like someone who's pretending anything."

Alone again, Michael considered his brother's words. Was Mark right? Had their friendship become something more real without him fully acknowledging it?

The thought both thrilled and terrified him. If he allowed himself to truly care for Anna—to hope for something beyond their temporary arrangement—what would happen when she returned to Ontario? Could he really ask her to give up her life, her work with her grandfather, her community, for the uncertainty of a relationship with him?

Another knock interrupted his spiraling thoughts. This time it was his father's voice. "Michael? Time for the meal."

"Coming," he called. Whatever his feelings might be, today he needed to focus on supporting Mark and Ellen's celebration. His own complicated emotions would have to wait.

Michael found his designated seat at the head table with the rest of the wedding party, while Anna sat with Emma and Drew several tables away. As was customary, they would not sit together until the evening meal—a tradition that suddenly seemed interminable.

Throughout the luncheon, Michael found his attention repeatedly drawn to Anna's table. She was engaged in animated conversation with Emma and several other women, her face bright with genuine enjoyment. Occasionally, she would glance in his direction, and their eyes would meet across the crowded space, creating a moment that, despite the crowd, felt intensely private.

He also noticed Leah and Heather together at a table with the Miller family. Rather than appearing disappointed or awkward, both women seemed to be thoroughly enjoying themselves. Heather was deep in conversation with one of Ellen's cousins from Lancaster—a young man Michael vaguely remembered meeting during the pre-wedding introductions. And Leah was laughing at something Joe had said, her face animated and happy.

Clearly, Ada and Sarah's matchmaking schemes had been more about the older women's enthusiasm than the younger women's actual interest. And he didn't find that surprising at all. He'd never been the type women flocked to.

As the meal concluded and preparations began for the afternoon activities, Michael made his way toward Anna's table. Now that the luncheon was almost over, they could spend the rest of the celebration together.

"How was your lunch?" he asked as he approached.

"Wonderful," Anna replied with genuine warmth. "I've never seen so much delicious food in one place."

"Wait until you see the wedding supper this evening," Michael said with a smile. "Lydia and my mother have been planning the menu for weeks."

As they walked together toward where the games were being organized, Michael noticed several community members watching them with approving smiles. His mother caught his eye from across the yard and nodded with obvious satisfaction. Even Bishop Nafzinger seemed pleased as he observed their interaction.

So far, Joel had been too preoccupied to notice. And Michael was glad. He wasn't sure what Joel would think if he knew the real direction Michael's heart was taking.

The weight expectations settled on his shoulders like a familiar burden.

"Michael?" Anna's voice drew him from his worried thoughts. "You look like you're carrying the weight of the world. Is everything all right?"

Her concern touched him deeply. Despite her own probable nervousness about the day, she was worried about his wellbeing.

"Just thinking about how public this all feels," he replied honestly.

Anna glanced around at the community gathering, her expression thoughtful. "It does feel like we're on display, doesn't it? But maybe that's not entirely bad."

"What do you mean?"

She was quiet for a moment, seeming to choose her words carefully. "Sometimes experiencing something helps you understand what the real thing might feel like."

Her observation hit closer to home than she probably realized. Michael studied her face, hoping they were both discovering the same reality. "I believe, Anna, that what's between us is real. Very real—"

Before he could explore the thought further, Samy appeared at their side with Sharon in tow. "The volleyball game is starting," she announced. "Emma saved spots for all of us on the same team."

"I agree." Anna whispered in his ear as they followed behind the two girls.

He was quite proud at that moment that he didn't trip over his own two feet. In fact, he may have simply floated on a cloud for the rest of their walk to the volleyball game.

As they moved toward the net, Michael caught sight of Leah standing with Joe, both cheering for the teams. The young man was explaining the rules to her with obvious enthusiasm, and Leah's attention was completely focused on him.

Nearby, Heather was helping organize the younger children into teams for their own games, working alongside several of the visiting young men who seemed charmed by her natural way with the children.

Perhaps, Michael thought with growing hope, this celebration would work out well for everyone involved, even if not in the ways originally planned.

As the afternoon games began and Anna laughed at something Emma said, Michael allowed himself to imagine, just for a moment, what it would be like if their relationship were real. The thought no longer seemed as impossible as it had just hours earlier.

Maybe Mark was right. Maybe the obstacles that seemed so insurmountable were simply challenges to be overcome, not walls to surrender behind.

The afternoon stretched ahead of them, full of possibility.

Chapter Eleven

Samy crouched low behind the oak tree, counting silently to herself as she watched the opposing team's flag flutter in the afternoon breeze. The capture-the-flag game had been Myles Beller's idea, and he'd divided the wedding guests into two teams with an air about him that made him seem all grown up. Samy wasn't sure how she felt about that. Did it mean he was too old to be her friend now? And was he here looking around for a girl to court, too?

Ach, she shook her head. No time to worry about that. She'd better pay attention to the game.

"Three guards by their flag," she whispered to Sharon, who was pressed against the tree beside her. "But there's a gap between the second and third oak trees if we're fast enough."

Sharon nodded, her eyes bright with excitement. Since arriving at the wedding celebration, she'd thrown herself into every activity with an enthusiasm that matched Samy's own. Having a friend who understood the importance of timing and planning made everything more enjoyable.

"On the count of three," Samy murmured, her muscles tensing for the sprint. "One... two..."

"Going somewhere, Samy Yoder?"

She spun around to find Myles standing behind them, his arms crossed and a knowing grin on his face. At eighteen, he had the advantage of height and longer legs, but Samy had been outrunning him across these fields since she was small enough to duck under his arm.

"Maybe," she replied, not giving away their plan. "Depends on whether you can catch us."

"Us?" Myles glanced at Sharon with interest. "I don't think we've been properly introduced. I'm Myles Beller."

"Sharon Fisher," Sharon replied with a shy smile. "We just moved here last month."

"The family with all the children," Myles nodded. "My *datt* mentioned you'd settled in Beulah Erb's old place. Are you enjoying New Hope?"

"Very much," Sharon answered. "Everyone's been so welcoming. Especially Samy."

Samy felt an unexpected flush of pride at Sharon's words. She'd never been anyone's first friend before, never been the one someone else depended on for social guidance. It was both gratifying and slightly terrifying.

"Well," Myles said, his attention returning to Samy, "if you think you can outrun me to that flag, you're welcome to try. But I've gotten faster since last summer."

"And I've gotten smarter," Samy retorted, then immediately took off running with Sharon close behind.

They made it past three trees before Myles caught up, his longer stride eating up the distance between them. But instead of tagging them out, he ran alongside them, occasionally calling out warnings about obstacles or opposing team members.

"Left!" he shouted as one of the Miller cousins appeared from behind a wagon. "And duck—low branch!"

Samy grinned despite the competition. This was why she'd always felt comfortable around Myles, even when kids her own age were frustrating to understand. Myles enjoyed games for the fun of it. He was never just about winning.

They reached the opposing team's territory together, and Myles held up a hand for them to stop. "Go get your flag," he said to Samy with a serious expression. "I got you here, but the capture has to be yours."

"Why?" Sharon asked, genuinely curious.

"Because if I know Samy, she already had a strategy before I showed up," Myles replied with a smile. "And because she's faster than both of us when it really counts."

The acknowledgment of her abilities warmed Samy more than she'd expected. Without another word, she darted from their hiding spot, snatched the flag from its post, and raced back toward home territory with Sharon and Myles flanking her like bodyguards.

The cheers from their teammates when they crossed the boundary line were satisfying, but not as much as the approving nod Myles gave her as he helped her up from where she'd tumbled in her victory slide.

"Good job," he said simply.

"Good teamwork," she replied, brushing grass from her dress.

As the games continued and teams reformed for different activities, Samy found herself moving between her friendship with Sharon and her easy camaraderie with Myles. It struck her that she had *two* friends—something that had always seemed impossible before.

"Samy," Sharon said during a break between games, "Myles is nice. Is he going to be in our class when school starts?"

"*Nay*," Samy replied, watching as Myles organized the younger children for a relay race. "He's too old for school. He works on his family's dairy farm now."

"Oh." Sharon looked thoughtful. "I'm surprised he pays any attention to us, then."

The observation surprised Samy. "Myles isn't like other boys. He's always been kind to me, even when other people thought I was..." She paused, searching for the right word.

"Different?" Sharon supplied gently.

"*Ya*. Different." Samy appreciated Sharon understood without her having to explain. "Myles never minded that I don't always understand things the way other people do."

"That's because he's a good person," Sharon said matter-of-factly. "And because being different isn't a bad thing. It's just... different."

Just then, a commotion near the volleyball net captured their attention. Michael and Anna were playing on the same team, and Anna had just made what appeared to be an excellent serve. The way Michael's face lit up with admiration was unmistakable, even to her.

"Look at them," Sharon said, following Samy's gaze. "They really do look like they're in love."

Samy studied the couple with the careful attention she usually reserved for watching horses. Michael's body language was relaxed and protective as he stood near Anna. When she laughed at something Emma said, his smile was automatic and genuine. And Anna... Anna kept glancing at Michael with an expression that Samy had seen before but couldn't immediately place.

Then it hit her. It was the same look Rachel Detweiler got when she watched Noah working with the therapy horses—a mixture of admiration, affection and something deeper that Samy didn't have words for.

"Sharon," she said slowly, "I think they forgot they're supposed to be pretending."

"What do you mean?"

Samy pointed discreetly toward the volleyball game. "Watch how they stand near each other. See Michael's face when Anna does something well. And watch Anna when she thinks no one is looking at her looking at Michael."

Sharon observed for several minutes, her expression growing more thoughtful. "You're right," she said finally. "That's not pretending. That's real."

"But they don't seem to know it yet," Samy added, frustrated by the adults' apparent inability to see what was obvious to her. "Or maybe they know, but they're scared of it."

"Why would they be scared?"

"Because it's complicated," Samy replied, remembering the conversations she'd overheard. "She's Mennonite, and he's Amish. And he's supposed to be focused on teaching. And she has to go back to Ontario."

Sharon was quiet for a moment, watching as Michael helped Anna up after she'd dove for a particularly difficult shot. The care in his movements and the way Anna's face softened as she thanked him made their feelings even more obvious.

"Maybe," Sharon said thoughtfully, "they just need to realize that the complicated stuff isn't as important as the real stuff."

Samy looked at her new friend with surprise. For someone who'd only known them for a few hours, Sharon had a remarkable understanding of the situation.

"You think they'll figure it out?" Samy asked.

"Eventually," Sharon replied with more confidence than Samy had on such things. "But they might need help."

"What kind of help?"

Sharon smiled, and Samy got a sense that her new friend was planning something particularly ambitious.

"The kind of help that makes them see what everyone else already knows," Sharon said. "But we'll have to be subtle about it. Adults don't like to think children are managing their love lives."

Samy grinned. Having a friend who also thought strategically was even better than she'd imagined. "I like the way you think, Sharon Fisher."

"And I like the way you see things, Samy Yoder."

As the afternoon games continued around them, the two girls began quietly planning an intervention that would help Michael and Anna recognize what their hearts already knew, even if their minds hadn't caught up yet.

After all, Samy reasoned, if adults could matchmake for their own purposes, surely *youngies* like them could do the same for better reasons.

Michael wiped sweat from his forehead as the volleyball game concluded, grateful that their team won despite his less-than-stellar performance. Around him, the wedding celebration continued with the easy joy that marked the best community gatherings—children running between groups of adults, elderly relatives sharing stories in the shade, young people planning the next activity.

But his attention was focused entirely on Anna, who was laughing breathlessly as Emma commiserated with her about a serve that had sailed well over the net and into the apple trees. The afternoon sun caught the strawberry highlights in her hair beneath her prayer covering, and her face glowed with the exertion and amusement of their shared athletic mishaps.

"Well, that was humbling," he said with a rueful grin as they walked toward the drink station. "I'm fairly certain I hit the ball backwards more often than forwards."

"At least you actually made contact with it," Anna replied with a laugh, accepting the glass of lemonade he offered. "I think I spent more time swinging at air than anything else. Though I haven't laughed this hard in years."

"Really?" The admission surprised him. "What do you usually do for fun in Ontario?"

Anna was quiet for a moment, sipping her lemonade thoughtfully. "I read mostly. Help at the museum. Sometimes Lois, Mary, and I go for walks or visit other towns' historical sites." She glanced up at him with a rueful smile. "It sounds rather quiet when I say it like that."

"Quiet isn't necessarily bad," Michael said gently. "But this suits you too. The games, the community celebration. You fit right in."

The observation was meant as a compliment, but he noticed Anna's expression grew more serious at his words.

"Do I?" she asked, her voice carrying an odd note. "I'm not sure anymore what is real and what is supposed to be pretend."

The comment hit very close to home. "What part feels real to you?"

Anna gestured toward the surrounding celebration. "All of this—being part of your family's joy, joining in the games, feeling like I belong here—it's wonderful. But it's also temporary. In a few days, I'll return to Ontario and my quiet life with my grandfather, and all of this will be like a lovely dream I had once."

The sadness in her voice caught him off guard. "It doesn't have to be temporary," he said before he could stop himself.

Anna's eyes widened slightly. "Doesn't it? Michael, we've been very careful not to examine too closely what's been happening between us, but we can't pretend forever that the obstacles aren't real."

Her directness forced him to confront the thoughts he'd been avoiding all day. "What obstacles do you mean, specifically?"

"Our different communities, for one," Anna replied, though her tone was more thoughtful than resigned. "Your commitment to teaching here, my responsibilities at the museum. The fact that we barely know each other outside of our translation correspondence."

"And yet," Michael said quietly, "here we are, and it doesn't feel like we're strangers."

"No," Anna agreed softly. "It doesn't."

"It all feels very real to me too, Anna" He took her hand, intending to hold it for the briefest second, but she didn't pull away.

They stood in comfortable silence for a moment, hands entwined, watching the ongoing activities around them. Near the croquet area, Michael spotted Leah engaged in animated conversation again with Joe Peters. The young man was clearly charmed and found her funny for he laughed often.

At the horseshoe pit, Heather was teaching several of the younger children the proper throwing technique, with one of Winston's cousins offering helpful commentary and obvious admiration for her patience with the little ones.

"Leah and Heather seem happy," Anna observed, following his gaze.

"They do," Michael agreed.

"Perhaps everyone is finding exactly what they need today," Anna said, her voice carrying a note of wonder.

Before Michael could respond to the implications of her statement, Samy and Sharon appeared at their side, both girls flushed with excitement and grass stains.

"Michael," Samy announced, "Sharon and I think you and Anna should enter the three-legged race."

"The what?" Anna asked, looking confused.

"It's starting in a few minutes," Sharon explained enthusiastically. "Two people tie their legs together and try to run as a team. Emma and Drew already signed up, and so did several other couples."

Michael glanced at Anna, unsure how she'd respond. To his delight, her eyes lit up with interest.

"That sounds like fun," she said. "Though I should warn you, Michael, coordinated activities might not be my strong suit."

"I find that reassuring rather than concerning," he replied with a smile, remembering his own fumbling attempts during the games. "At least we'll be equally uncoordinated."

"In that case," Anna said with a smile that made his heart skip, "we should do very well."

As they made their way toward the starting line, Michael caught sight of several church members watching them with approving smiles. His mother looked positively delighted, and even his *datt* nodded with what appeared to be satisfaction.

"Oh, look!" Sharon pointed excitedly toward the growing group of participants. "It's not all couples. See there, I think those two are sisters. Samy, we should enter too!"

Samy's eyes lit up at the suggestion. "Would you want to? I've never done a three-legged race before."

"Neither have I, but it looks like fun," Sharon replied. "And we work well together."

Nearby, Myles was attempting to convince his brother Martin to join him. "Come on, Martin. It's just for fun."

"Easy for you to say," Martin grumbled good-naturedly. "You're not the one who tripped over his own feet during capture the flag."

"It's only for fun," Myles grinned. "I see Michael is joining. My expectations were low, but I think we can be guaranteed at least not to come in last, now."

As the participants gathered at the starting line, Michael found himself in good company. Emma and Drew were already tied together and practicing their stride with mixed results. The older Weaver couple who'd been married for forty years stood with the patient confidence of people who'd spent decades moving in harmony. Several other wedding guests were laughing as they attempted practice steps.

Michael watched with amusement as one of the race organizers tied his and Anna's legs together with a soft rope. Standing this close to her, their sides pressed together, he was acutely aware of her warmth and the faint scent of lavender that always seemed to surround her.

"Ready?" Anna asked, her hand resting lightly on his arm for balance.

"As ready as someone can be for inevitable humiliation," he replied with a grin.

The starting signal came, and chaos immediately ensued. Michael and Anna managed exactly three steps before their lack of coordination sent them stumbling sideways into Drew and Emma, creating a domino effect that took down two other couples.

Meanwhile, Samy and Sharon moved with surprising synchronization, their friendship translating into an intuitive understanding of each other's movements. They pulled ahead of the pack while most other teams were still struggling to find their rhythm.

"Left, left, right, left," Samy called quietly to Sharon, and they adjusted their pace perfectly.

Behind them, Myles and Martin were making steady progress despite Martin's predictions of disaster. "What did I tell you?" Myles called to his brother as they gained ground. "We're not last!"

That distinction belonged to Michael and Anna, who had managed to travel roughly ten feet before stopping to dissolve into laughter.

"I think," Anna gasped between giggles, "we should focus on not falling down rather than winning."

"Ambitious goals," Michael agreed, helping to steady them both. "Should we try again?"

They began a shuffling progress toward the finish line, their "running" more resembling an enthusiastic walk. Around them, other couples were having varying degrees of success, but Michael found he didn't care how far away they were from the finish line. The sound of Anna's laughter and the way she squeezed his arm when they nearly toppled again was worth more than any victory.

Samy and Sharon crossed the finish line first, their teamwork having served them well throughout the race. They raised their joined hands in triumph while the crowd cheered.

"We did it!" Sharon exclaimed, beaming with pride.

"We make a good team," Samy agreed, her face glowing with the satisfaction of a well-executed plan.

Emma and Drew crossed the line in second place, if slightly disheveled. Myles and Martin came in third, both brothers grinning despite Martin's earlier protests. And then the Weaver couple finished with dignified grace, while the other teams came behind them.

Michael and Anna brought up the rear, but they were laughing too hard to care about their last place finish.

"That was thoroughly embarrassing," Anna announced cheerfully as someone untied their legs. "And absolutely wonderful."

"We should definitely stick to academic pursuits," Michael agreed, still catching his breath from laughter. "Though I have to admit, losing has never been so enjoyable."

Standing beside Anna as they congratulated Samy and Sharon on their victory, he felt a sense of rightness that had nothing to do with community expectations and everything to do with the woman beside him.

And Anna seemed to feel the same. The question was what they were going to do about it.

C hapter Twelve

The afternoon sun was beginning its descent toward the horizon when the call came for everyone to gather for the evening meal. Michael felt a flutter of nervous anticipation as he realized the moment had arrived. He and Anna would officially sit together as a couple.

Around them, the wedding celebration reorganized itself with the efficiency of a community accustomed to large gatherings. Tables were rearranged, additional benches brought out, and the carefully planned seating assignments that would formally pair couples took shape.

"Michael," his mother approached with a warm smile, "you and Anna are at the head table, three seats down from Mark and Ellen."

The placement was significant—close enough to the bride and groom to honor Michael's role as brother but positioned as a couple in their own right. Michael nodded his understanding, then went to find Anna, who was helping clear the remains of the afternoon's activities.

"Time for the evening meal," he said, offering his arm with a formality that felt both natural and nerve-wracking.

"Already?" Anna glanced around at the bustling preparations. "The day has flown by so quickly."

As they walked toward the head table, Michael noticed the subtle but unmistakable attention their approach garnered. Conversations paused momentarily as they passed, and he caught glimpses of approving nods and satisfied smiles looking their way. The weight of their expectations settled on his shoulders, but for once it felt less like pressure and more like... hope. Their hopes for him and Anna encouraged a new hope of his own.

At their assigned seats, Michael helped Anna settle before taking his place beside her. The intimacy of the arrangement—sitting close enough that their shoulders nearly touched, sharing the same general space in a way that proclaimed their partnership to everyone present—sent a surprising warmth through his chest.

"How are you feeling?" he asked quietly as the other guests found their places.

"Nervous," Anna admitted with a small smile. "But in a good way, I think. Like when you're about to embark on an adventure you've been looking forward to."

Her words resonated with something deep in Michael's heart. That was exactly how he felt—as though he stood on the threshold of something significant and wonderful, even if he couldn't yet see its full shape.

As the meal began with Bishop Nafzinger's blessing, Michael found himself increasingly aware of Anna beside him. The way she listened attentively to the conversations around their table, contributing thoughtful observations, and the genuine warmth with which she responded to questions and comments.

"Anna," Mattie leaned across the table from her seat with Winston, "Michael mentioned you work at a museum. What's your favorite piece in the collection?"

Anna's face lit up with enthusiasm. "We have a quilt that was made by a group of Mennonite women during their journey to Canada in 1874. Each woman contributed a square that represented something from their homeland they had to leave behind. The stories embedded in that quilt... they never fail to move me."

"How beautiful," Ellen said from further down the table. "Preserving those memories for future generations—that's such important work."

"It is," Anna agreed. "Though sometimes I wonder if there are more ways to bring those stories to life, to help people connect with their heritage beyond just seeing artifacts behind glass."

Michael studied Anna's profile as she spoke, noting the passion that animated her features when she discussed her work.

"You could teach," he said. "Share those stories in schools, churches, community centers. Make history come alive for people who might never visit a museum."

Anna turned to look at him, surprise flickering in her eyes. "You're the second person to make that suggestion since I've been here. Do you think I could? I mean would schools like your welcome that kind of special instruction?"

"I certainly would advocate for it," Michael replied with quiet conviction. "You'd probably be welcomed in many schools, not only ours."

The conversation was interrupted by Mark rising to thank all the guests who had traveled to share in their celebration. As his brother continues to express his gratitude to everyone present, Michael felt Anna's hand brush against his on the table. Whether intentional or accidental, the brief contact sent warmth shooting up his arm.

As the evening progressed and conversation flowed around their table, Michael found himself drawn into a bubble of contentment he hadn't expected. The combination of family celebration, community fellowship and Anna's presence beside him created a sense of completeness he'd never experienced before.

During a lull in conversation while dessert was being served, Anna leaned slightly closer to him. "Thank you," she said quietly.

"For what?"

"For today. For including me in all of this. For making me feel like I belong here." Her voice carried a note of wonder. "I haven't felt this... connected since I was very young."

The wistfulness in her tone tugged at something in Michael's chest. "You do belong here," he said, the words emerging with more intensity than he'd intended. "I can't imagine this day without you."

Anna's breath caught slightly at his declaration, and for a moment they simply looked at each other, the noise and activity of the celebration fading into background.

It was then, in that moment of shared recognition, that Michael made a decision that felt both inevitable and terrifying. Slowly, deliberately, he reached under the table and found Anna's hand where it rested on her lap. Their fingers intertwined with a natural ease that sent warmth radiating through his entire body.

Anna's eyes widened slightly at the contact, but she didn't pull away. Instead, her fingers tightened around his, and a soft smile curved her lips—the kind of smile that was meant for him alone.

They sat like that for the remainder of the meal, hands linked beneath the white tablecloth, participating in the other conversations around them while also sharing a private connection that felt more real than anything Michael had ever experienced. The weight of her trust, the warmth of her acceptance, the rightness of her presence beside him. It all crystallized into a moment of perfect clarity.

This was what he wanted. Not just for today, not just to avoid matchmaking schemes, but for always. Anna Roth, with her quick mind and gentle spirit, her passion for preserving the past and her dreams of sharing it with others. He wanted to build a life with her, to support her ambitions while pursuing his own, to create the kind of partnership his brother had found with Ellen.

The realization should have terrified him. Instead, it filled him with a peace and certainty that made all those obstacles seem surmountable.

As the meal concluded and people began preparing for the evening's singing, Michael squeezed Anna's hand gently.

"Whatever happens after today," he said quietly, "I want you to know that this has been the best day of my life."

Anna's smile in response was radiant, full of joy and something that looked remarkably like love.

Neither of them noticed Leah Erb watching from across the room, her expression thoughtful as she observed their obvious connection. Nor did they see her leaning over to whisper something to Joe Peters, whose eyebrows rose in surprise at whatever she shared.

The seeds of complication were already being sown, even as Michael and Anna sat basking in their newfound certainty about each other.

Anna felt as though she were floating as the evening meal concluded around her. Michael's hand remained linked with hers beneath the table, his thumb occasionally brushing across her knuckles in a gesture that sent shivers of warmth up her arm. The conversations swirling around their table seemed to come from a great distance, filtered through the haze of contentment that had settled over her.

She had agreed to attend this wedding as Michael's pretend companion, armed with careful plans to maintain boundaries and return to Ontario with her emotions intact. Instead, she found herself falling deeper into something that felt suspiciously like love with each passing hour.

The realization should have frightened her. Should have sent her practical mind spinning with concerns about the impossible nature of their situation. Instead, all she could focus on was the rightness of Michael's presence beside her, the way their conversation flowed as naturally as breathing, the sense of homecoming she felt whenever he smiled at her.

"Anna?" Emma's voice drew her attention. "We were just discussing the singing that's about to begin. Will you be joining us?"

"Oh, yes," Anna replied, trying to refocus on the present conversation. "I'm looking forward to it."

"I love a good hymn sing," Heather added from her seat at a nearby table. She'd been paired with James Miller for the evening meal, and both seemed pleased with the arrangement. "All the voices joining together in harmony—it's one of my favorite parts of any celebration."

Anna nodded, though she wondered if she'd be able to concentrate on singing when Michael was sitting beside her. The awareness of his presence had become almost overwhelming in the most wonderful way possible.

As people began clearing the tables and rearranging seating for the evening's music, Michael finally released her hand. The separation felt like a loss, and when he offered his arm to escort her to the singing area, she accepted it gratefully.

"You're quiet," he observed as they found seats on one of the benches arranged in a large circle. "Having second thoughts about... the singing? I don't claim to be the best. Perhaps you should sit further away."

Anna smiled at his gentle teasing. "Not second thoughts. But I should warn you that my friends say I am tone deaf. You may wish to sit further away from me."

"Never." His adamance bolstered her spirits.

"Honestly, I was just... processing everything." While she was being honest, she may as well go all in. "Today has been more wonderful than I could have imagined."

Michael's expression grew serious. "For me as well. Anna, I hope you know that what's happening between us—"

"Is real," she finished softly. "Yes, I know. I feel it too."

The simple acknowledgment hung between them, heavy with implications neither was quite ready to fully examine. Around them, everyone was settling into the familiar rhythm of an old-fashioned hymn sing, but Anna felt as though she and Michael existed in their own private world.

The singing began, voices blending in the four-part harmony that was the hallmark of both Amish and Mennonite musical traditions. Anna was drawn in, overcome by the power of their voices and the age-old words that unified them.

As the evening progressed and the music moved from hymns to folk songs to more playful tunes, Anna relaxed completely for perhaps the first time in years. The combination of music and Michael's steady presence beside her created a sense of belonging she couldn't have known she'd been missing.

The weight of everyone's earlier assumptions no longer pressed against Anna's consciousness, because it no longer felt like deception. Whatever had begun as pretense had transformed into something genuine and precious. The obstacles that had seemed insurmountable just days ago—their different communities, her responsibilities in Ontario, his commitment to teaching here—suddenly seemed like puzzles to be solved rather than walls to surrender behind.

"What are you thinking about?" Michael asked quietly during a pause between songs.

"The future," Anna replied honestly. "All the possibilities I never let myself consider before."

His smile in response was soft and full of promise. "I've been thinking about that too. We'll figure it out, Anna. Whatever it takes, we'll find a way."

The certainty in his voice made her heart soar. Yes, they would find a way. Love this strong, this right, didn't come along often enough to be carelessly dismissed due to practical concerns.

As the evening wound down, Anna was reluctant for the day to end. Tomorrow would bring the return of ordinary life, time to think and plan and worry about the complications they would face. Tonight, she wanted to hold on to the magic they had discovered.

"Walk with me?" Michael asked as the final song concluded and people began to disperse.

"Always," Anna replied without hesitation.

As they made their way toward a quieter area of the farm, neither noticed Leah Erb speaking earnestly with her host family, gesturing occasionally in their direction. Nor did they see the concerned expressions that crossed her Aunt Sarah's face as Leah spoke.

The perfect day was about to become more complicated than either Michael or Anna could imagine. But for now, in the gentle darkness of a Prince Edward Island evening, they walked hand in hand toward a future that seemed filled with endless possibility.

C hapter Thirteen

Michael walked with Anna along the quiet path that wound behind the Beller farmhouse, their hands still linked, the sounds of the celebration growing distant behind them. The evening air was soft and warm, filled with the scent of honeysuckle and the gentle sounds of crickets beginning their nightly chorus.

"It's beautiful here," Anna said softly, looking up at the first stars appearing in the darkening sky. "I can understand why your community chose this place."

"It has a way of growing on you," Michael agreed, though his attention was focused more on Anna's profile in the twilight than on the familiar landscape around them. "Sometimes I think the island chooses its people as much as people choose it."

Anna turned to smile at him, and Michael felt his breath catch at the tenderness in her expression. "Is that what happened to you? The island chose you?"

"Oh, I don't know about that, but I do know that *Gott's* ways are more than I can ever understand," he replied, surprised by the certainty in his own voice. "The decisions that brought me here—my family's choice to move—that wasn't my doing. But everything since... my decision to teach, even my impulsive email invitation—it all led to this moment. It all brought me here with you. And it doesn't feel like I can take credit for that, either. This," he put an arm around her shoulders, "This is far too wonderful for that."

The romantic sentiment hung between them in the gathering darkness, and Michael warmed as Anna lean against him, fitting perfectly beside him. He was about to voice more of the thoughts that had been building throughout the evening when the sound of approaching footsteps interrupted them.

"Michael?" Joel Yoder's voice carried clearly in the still air. "Might I have a word with you?"

Michael's heart sank at the serious tone in Joel's voice. Whatever had prompted this interruption, it wasn't a casual social call. "Of course," he replied, though he was reluctant to release Anna's hand.

"Anna," Joel nodded politely to her, "Lydia is looking for you to help with the cleanup. She's by the kitchen area."

The dismissal was gentle but clear. Anna looked between the two men, obviously sensing the tension in the air. "Of course," she said. "Michael, I'll... I'll see you later?"

The question in her voice made Michael's chest tighten. "Yes," he assured her. "We'll talk soon."

After Anna disappeared toward the farmhouse, Joel stood in silence for a moment, his expression thoughtful in the dim light.

"Beautiful evening," he said finally.

"Yes," Michael agreed, though his stomach was knotting with apprehension. "The celebration has been wonderful. Mark and Ellen couldn't have hoped for more."

Joel clasped his hands behind his back, a gesture Michael recognized as the one he used when preparing to deliver difficult news or counsel. "Michael, I need to speak with you about a concern that's been brought to my attention."

Michael's mouth went dry. "What kind of concern?"

"About the nature of your relationship with Anna." Joel's voice remained calm and measured. "Sarah Erb approached Lydia this evening with some concerns."

Heat flooded Michael's face. "What kind of concerns?"

"The kind that suggest your feelings for Anna may have developed beyond what you originally intended." Joel paused, studying Michael's expression in the dim light. "She mentioned seeing you holding hands during the singing, the way you look at each other, the obvious affection between you."

Michael opened his mouth to deny it, then stopped. What was the point? It was all was true. "I can't deny that." He paused. "Although I'm not sure why it would concern Sarah. Those mothers have been trying to match make for months."

Joel sighed, and for the first time, Michael heard something like sympathy in his voice. "Sarah's reasons have more to do with Leah and her own family concerns... well, her brother Albert's really. All that goes way back and isn't your concern."

"I don't understand."

"It's because of Sarah's keen observations, and her apparent need to share them, that I realized you and I need to talk. Sooner rather than later, apparently. Michael, you're about to begin your first term as our schoolteacher. The community has placed tremendous trust in you, expecting you to provide stability and continuity for our children's education."

"I understand that," Michael replied, his voice tighter than he'd intended. "But I don't see how my personal feelings affect my ability to teach."

"Don't you?" Joel's question was gentle but pointed. "Anna is Mennonite, not Amish. She lives in Ontario and has responsibilities there with her grandfather's museum. If you pursue a courtship with her, one of you would need to make significant sacrifices. Either she leaves her community and life's work to join ours, or you leave your teaching position and the community that's counting on you."

The stark reality of Joel's words wasn't new, and yet they hit Michael like a physical blow. In his euphoria over the evening's developments, he hadn't been willing to face the practical implications of what pursuing Anna would mean.

Michael felt the ground shifting beneath his feet. "Are you saying the school board would withdraw their offer if I pursue a relationship with Anna?"

Joel was quiet for a long moment. "I'm saying that the board selected you partly because you seemed settled, focused on your calling as a teacher rather than distracted by romantic complications. If your situation changes dramatically, they would need to reconsider whether you're still the right choice for the position."

The words felt like a punch to Michael's stomach. The teaching position wasn't just a job to him—it was his calling, his way of serving the community, his path to making a meaningful contribution beyond dairy farming.

"And if Anna were to convert?" he asked, grasping for solutions. "If she joined our community?"

"That would certainly be different," Joel acknowledged. "But Michael, be honest with yourself. You know that most times this works the opposite way. It is difficult to go from progressive Mennonite to Amish, even if we are a more lenient district. Would Anna truly be happy here? Leaving her grandfather, her life's work, everything familiar to her?"

The questions struck at the heart of Michael's growing doubts. Throughout the evening, he'd been so focused on how right everything felt with Anna that he hadn't seriously considered what pursuing that feeling would cost her.

"I see you're beginning to understand the complexity of the situation," Joel said quietly. "I don't say this to hurt you, Michael. I can see that your feelings for Anna are genuine, and from what I've observed, hers for you are as well. But sometimes caring for someone means considering what's truly best for them, even when it's not what we want."

Michael stared out into the darkness, his mind reeling. "So what are you suggesting I do?"

"I'm suggesting you think carefully about what path you choose from here," Joel replied. "If you decide to pursue Anna seriously, you need to be prepared for the consequences that decision will bring—for both of you, and for our community. And you need to be honest with her about those consequences, so she can make an informed choice as well."

The weight of responsibility settled on Michael's shoulders like a heavy blanket. "And if I decide that the costs are too high?"

"Then you'll need to find a way to end this before either of you gets more deeply hurt than necessary." Joel's voice carried genuine regret. "I know that's not what you want to hear, Michael. But sometimes the right choice isn't the easy one."

As Joel's footsteps receded toward the farmhouse, Michael stood alone in the darkness, his earlier euphoria completely shattered. The magical evening he'd shared with Anna now felt like a cruel tease—a glimpse of something beautiful that was ultimately beyond his reach.

He thought about Anna's face during the singing, the joy and belonging he'd seen there. But did that mean he ought to ask her to give up everything she knew and loved in Ontario for a future here? And if not, how could he abandon his teaching position and the trust the community had placed in him?

The sound of laughter drifted from the farmhouse, where the cleanup was apparently proceeding with good cheer. But Michael felt no desire to return to the celebration. Instead, he began walking the familiar paths of his childhood, trying to find a way forward that wouldn't destroy everything he'd thought he wanted.

By the time he returned to the house, most of the guests had departed. Anna was nowhere to be seen, and when he asked his mother about her, Belinda simply said that Lydia had taken her home earlier, mentioning that Anna seemed tired.

Michael suspected there was more to Anna's departure than fatigue, but he was too emotionally drained to pursue the matter. Instead, he helped finish the cleanup in silence, his earlier joy replaced by a growing dread about the conversation he would eventually need to have with Anna.

The perfect day had ended with the sobering reminder of the practical realities of their two very different lives. As Michael finally made his way to his room, he couldn't shake the feeling that he'd been given a glimpse of paradise only to discover it was built on impossibly shifting sand.

Anna sat on the edge of her bed in the Yoder household, still wearing her good dress but with her head covering set aside for the night. The house was quiet around her—Samy was already asleep in the next bed, exhausted from the day's excitement, and the rest of the family had retired soon after their return from the Bellers.

But sleep eluded Anna. Her mind kept replaying the events of the evening, particularly the abrupt way it had ended. One moment she'd been walking hand-in-hand with Michael, feeling as though the whole world was full of possibility. The next, Joel had requested to speak with Michael privately, and shortly after, Lydia had appeared to escort her home with murmured explanations about the late hour and how tired she looked.

The transition had been so sudden and unexpected that Anna felt disoriented, as though she'd been jolted awake from a wonderful dream only to find herself back in harsh reality.

"Anna?" Samy's voice was barely above a whisper in the darkness. "Are you alright?"

Anna turned toward the other bed, surprised to find Samy awake. "I thought you were asleep."

"I was, but you keep moving around." Samy sat up, her red hair tousled from sleep. "Did something happen?"

The perceptive question reminded Anna of why she'd grown so fond of this unusual girl. Samy saw things others missed, and she wasn't afraid to ask direct questions.

"I'm not entirely sure," Anna replied honestly. "Joel wanted to speak with Michael privately, and then your mother brought me home. I couldn't help but feel like something had changed."

Samy was quiet for a moment, and Anna could almost hear her thinking in the darkness.

"Maybe someone said something," Samy said finally. "People were watching you and Michael all evening. And *Aenti* Sarah, well, she has a knack for stirring up trouble. *Mamm* says so, so I know it's true, even though I wasn't supposed to hear it. Well, if she got a bee in her bonnet over you and Michael, then..."

The blunt observation made Anna's stomach clench. "Was it that obvious? Michael and I?"

"To anyone who was looking, *ya*," Samy replied matter-of-factly. "The way you held hands during the singing, how you smiled at each other during supper. Sharon and I could tell, so probably everyone else could too."

Anna closed her eyes, trying to process the implications. If their genuine feelings had been so apparent, then perhaps someone had questioned Michael about his intentions. Given the complex circumstances of their situation—her Mennonite background, her life in Ontario, his new teaching position—such questions could quickly become problematic.

"Samy," she said quietly, "what do you know about the expectations for Michael as the new teacher?"

"You mean about not getting married right away?" Samy's directness was both helpful and unsettling. "I heard my *datt* and the bishop talking about it once. They said they chose Michael partly because he seemed focused on teaching instead of courting."

Anna's heart sank. "I see."

"But that was before you came," Samy added quickly. "Before they saw how happy you make him. Surely that changes things?"

The hope in Samy's voice made Anna's chest tight. "Perhaps. Or perhaps it makes things more complicated."

They sat in silence for several minutes; each lost in their own thoughts. Finally, Samy spoke again.

"Anna? Are you going to stay? Even if it's difficult?"

The question cut straight to the heart of Anna's confusion. Just hours ago, she would have said yes without hesitation. The connection she felt with Michael, the sense of belonging she'd discovered in his community, the possibility of building a life together—all of it had seemed worth fighting for.

But now, in the quiet darkness with reality pressing in around her, the obstacles loomed much larger. Her grandfather needed her. The museum was her life's work. She had responsibilities awaiting her return to Ontario.

And if Michael's teaching position was threatened by their relationship, she would never want to cause him to lose his calling to teach.

"I don't know," she whispered finally. "I honestly don't know."

Samy didn't respond, but Anna heard her settle back into her bed with a small sigh that sounded much older than her fourteen years.

As the night stretched on and sleep continued to elude her, Anna found herself questioning everything that had seemed so clear just hours before. Love might not be enough to bridge the gap between two very different lives, especially when pursuing it could cost Michael everything he'd worked toward.

Maybe the most loving thing she could do was walk away before anyone got hurt beyond repair. The thought made her heart ache, but she couldn't deny its logic.

Tomorrow, she would need to have a conversation with Michael that might change everything between them. Tonight, she could only lie in the darkness and wonder how foolish she'd been to believe that fairy tales could come true in real life.

C hapter Fourteen

Michael spread the handwritten pages of the nineteenth-century journal across the kitchen table, trying to focus on the Ukrainian passages that had puzzled him for weeks. The morning light streaming through the window should have been perfect for translation work, but the words seemed to blur together on the page.

Without Anna's meticulous notes and insightful questions, the work felt hollow and purposeless. He'd thought he could immerse himself in work and forget, temporarily at least, the impossible situation they found themselves in. Instead, every sentence he translated reminded him of her absence.

"Michael?" His mother's voice interrupted his futile concentration. "You've been staring at that same page for twenty minutes."

He looked up to find Belinda studying him with the concerned expression she'd worn since he'd returned from his walk with Joel two days ago. Word had spread quickly through the family that something had gone wrong between him and Anna, though he'd been vague about the details.

"Just a difficult passage," he replied, though they both knew that wasn't the real problem.

Belinda set a cup of coffee beside him and settled into the adjacent chair. "Son, I've seen you work through translations that would probably stump *Englischer* university professors. This isn't about difficult Ukrainian grammar."

Michael set down his pen and rubbed his temples. His mother was right, of course. The journal work that had once energized him now felt like a meaningless puzzle. Every insight he wanted to share, every question that arose, every moment of discovery—all of it felt incomplete without Anna there to share it with him.

"I've made a mess of things, *Mamm*," he admitted quietly.

"Have you?" Belinda's voice carried a gentle challenge. "Or have you simply discovered that some things matter more than you realized?"

Michael looked at his mother with surprise. "I thought you'd be disappointed. The teaching position, the community's expectations—"

"Michael," Belinda interrupted gently, "your father and I have been married for thirty-one years. Do you think we don't recognize genuine love when we see it?"

The words hit him like a physical blow. "But the complications—"

"Can be worked through if both people care enough to try." Belinda reached across the table to cover his hand with hers. "The question isn't whether there are obstacles. The question is whether you're going to let fear keep you from fighting for something precious."

"Joel made it clear that pursuing Anna could cost me the teaching position."

"Joel also said the situation would be different if Anna joined our community," Belinda pointed out. "Did you even explore that possibility with her?"

Michael felt heat rise in his cheeks. "No. I couldn't ask her to make such a sacrifice."

"Don't you think that should be her choice?"

The gentle reproach in his mother's voice made Michael realize how presumptuous he'd been. In his effort to protect Anna, he'd denied her the chance to make her own future—to follow *Gott's* leading in her own heart.

"I was trying to protect her," he said weakly.

"I understand. And that is honorable of you, but..." Belinda shook her head. "*Sohn*, Anna is an intelligent, capable woman. Don't you think you can trust her to make her own decisions about what sacrifices she's willing to make?"

Michael stared down at the journal pages and saw Anna's careful handwriting in the margins of an earlier entry and recalled her excitement when they'd made breakthrough discoveries together.

"I think I've been a fool," he mumbled.

"Perhaps," Belinda agreed with a small smile. "But it's not too late to remedy that."

Before Michael could respond, the sound of horse hooves in the yard drew their attention. Through the window, they could see Samy Yoder dismounting from Amazon near the barn, a small package in her hand.

"Expecting Samy?" Belinda asked.

"No," Michael replied, rising from the table. Something about Samy's purposeful movements suggested this wasn't a casual visit.

He met her halfway across the yard, noting the determined expression on her usually reserved face.

"Samy," he greeted her. "This is a surprise."

"I came to return this," she said, holding out what appeared to be a book. "Myles loaned it to me last week."

Michael glanced toward the barn where his brothers were working. "He's inside with the morning milking."

"Actually," Samy said, her direct gaze fixing on his face, "I was hoping to talk to you first."

The unusual request caught Michael off guard. "About what?"

Samy glanced around as if to see who else might hear, then spoke with her characteristic bluntness. "About how miserable Anna has been since the wedding."

Michael felt heat rise in his cheeks. "Samy, that's not really—"

"She cried yesterday," Samy interrupted. "Anna doesn't seem like someone who cries easily, but she was trying to hide it while helping my *mamm* in the *shoppe*. And..." she gave him a looking over, "you look like you haven't slept much."

The accurate observation left Michael with no ready defense. "It's complicated, Samy."

"Most good things are hard," she replied, echoing something Myles had said recently. "But that doesn't mean you give up on them."

"There are things you can't understand—"

"Like what?" Samy's directness was unrelenting. "That she's Mennonite and you're Amish? That she lives in Ontario, and you live here? That people might disapprove?"

"Those aren't small problems, Samy."

"No, they're not," she agreed. "But they're not impossible either. Rachel Erb married Noah Detweiler even though he'd left the Amish. But he came back, didn't he? And he is happy here. Ellen joined the Mennonite church to marry Mark. People find ways when they care enough."

Michael stared at this fourteen-year-old girl who seemed to possess wisdom far beyond her years. "And what makes you think Anna and I *care enough*?" He chose her words, though they weren't nearly strong enough for what he felt.

"Because I have eyes," Samy replied matter-of-factly. "I saw how you looked at each other during the wedding, how you both lit up when you were together. And you know that if I noticed, it had to be obvious. Of course, it helped that Sharon pointed it out often enough."

"I see." Despite everything, Michael held back a chuckle at Samy's explanation.

Samy thrust a hand on her hip, not liking that he was amused. "And, Michael Beller, because Anna

229

talks about you even when she's trying not to. Being scared isn't a good reason to give up on something wonderful."

Michael felt something shift inside him at her words. "When did you become so wise about matters of the heart?"

"When I started learning that sometimes you have to step outside what feels safe to find what makes you happy," Samy replied. "Making friends with Sharon was scary for me. But if I'd stayed safe in my routine, I would have missed out on something really good."

The parallel between her situation and his was startling. Michael looked at this girl who'd struggled with social connections her entire life yet had found the courage to embrace a new friendship despite her fears.

"Samy," he said quietly, "has Anna said anything about... about what she might want?"

"She said she's never felt like she belonged anywhere the way she felt she belonged here," Samy replied. "She said being part of our community felt like coming home to a place she'd never been before."

Michael felt his heart start to race. "She said that?"

"Yesterday, while we were doing the supper dishes. She also said she keeps thinking about all the ways history could come alive for school children." Samy paused, studying his face. "Sounds like someone who'd like to stay here to me."

The possibility that Anna might genuinely want to build a life here, that her feelings might be strong enough to overcome the practical obstacles, sent hope surging through Michael's chest.

"Thank you, Samy," he said sincerely. "For caring enough to come here, for being brave enough to speak honestly."

"Just don't waste it," she replied with characteristic directness, as she walked toward the barn to find Myles,

Michael felt as though the world had shifted beneath his feet. Perhaps his mother and Samy were right. Perhaps he'd been so focused on protecting Anna from difficult choices that he'd forgotten to trust her to make them.

The journal translation could wait. Some conversations were more important than academic work, and this was one of them.

Anna sat on the front porch of the Yoder house, mechanically snapping green beans for the evening meal while her mind wandered to places it shouldn't go. Every task felt hollow without the anticipation of sharing the day's experiences with Michael. Every moment of beauty—the play of light on the fields, the sound of children's laughter from a neighboring farm, the satisfaction of useful work—felt incomplete without someone who would understand why it mattered.

She'd been in New Hope for almost a week, and already the thought of returning to Ontario filled her with a sadness she couldn't fully explain. Not just because of Michael, though his absence from her days felt like a missing piece of herself. But because this place, this community, had awakened something in her she hadn't known was sleeping.

"You've snapped those beans to pieces," Samy observed, settling beside her on the porch steps.

Anna looked down at the bowl in her lap and realized she'd been breaking the beans into fragments much smaller than necessary. "I suppose I was distracted."

"By thoughts of home?" Samy asked, though her tone suggested she knew the answer.

"By thoughts of where home actually is," Anna replied honestly.

Samy studied her with those perceptive eyes that seemed to see more than they should. "And where is that?"

Anna gestured all around them. "I keep thinking it might be here. Which might seem ridiculous, considering I've only been here a week."

"Maybe not." Samy said. "Sometimes you know right away when something fits, just like you know right away when it doesn't."

The simple observation made Anna smile despite her melancholy. "Is that how you felt about Sharon?"

"*Ya*," Samy replied without hesitation. "The first time we really talked, I knew she understood things about me that other people don't. That doesn't happen often."

"No, it doesn't," Anna agreed, thinking of Michael and the immediate connection she'd felt with him from their very first conversation.

"Are you sad because you have to leave, or because you think you have to leave?" Samy asked with characteristic directness.

The question forced Anna to examine her assumptions. "What do you mean?"

"I mean, maybe the choice isn't as impossible as you think it is."

Anna set down the bowl of beans and turned to face Samy fully. "What do you know about my choice?"

"I know you're miserable," Samy replied matter-of-factly. "I know Michael is miserable too. You're both acting like your only options are being apart or causing disaster for everyone."

"Well now, that about sums it up." Anna laughed. "And sounds quite ridiculous when put that way. But it's not that simple, Samy. Michael's teaching position, my responsibilities to my grandfather—"

"Might all be more flexible than you think," Samy interrupted. "But you'll never know if you keep assuming the worst about everything. Mamm tells me that all the time, when I get afraid of anything new or different."

The blunt assessment stung because it contained so much truth. Anna realized she had been assuming the worst—that pursuing her feelings for Michael would inevitably lead to disappointment and sacrifice that neither of them could handle.

"Thank you, Samy. You've given me some things to really thing about." Anna answered quietly.

Anna stared out across the fields toward the Beller farm, where Michael was presumably going about his daily routine as if his world hadn't been turned upside down. Just as she was going about hers.

She was scared, she realized, probably much in the way that the world often intimidated Samy. And her instinct was to run from those fears. But hadn't she learned from her parents' abandonment that running wasn't how she wanted to respond?

"You're very clever for fourteen," Anna said softly.

"Sometimes being different from other people means you see things they miss," Samy replied. "I sure hope you stay, Anna. I think we will all miss out on a lot of things if you don't."

"Oh, Samy," Anna felt her heart might burst. "I am so glad to know you."

"So, that's all I have to say about that. I have to go now." Samy's mission complete, she headed toward the barn to fetch Amazon for her afternoon visit to Noah's farm.

Anna laughed softly at Samy's sudden exit and continued to snap the rest of the beans. When had a teenage girl become one of the wisest people she knew? And when had she become too much of a coward to fight for what she wanted?

The question terrified and exhilarated her in equal measure. But as she looked out across the landscape that was beginning to feel like home, Anna knew Samy was right. Some risks were worth taking, especially when the alternative was a lifetime of regret.

Tomorrow, she would find the courage to have a conversation with Michael that might change everything. Tonight, she would allow herself to hope that love might be stronger than fear after all.

Chapter Fifteen

Michael found Anna in the early morning light, sitting on the wooden bench beneath the large oak tree behind the Yoder house. She held a cup of coffee in her hands, steam rising in the cool air, and her gaze was fixed on the distant horizon where the sun was painting the sky in soft pastels.

She must have heard his footsteps on the grass, but she didn't turn around before speaking. "I wondered if you might come," she said.

"I've waited too long to come," Michael replied, settling beside her on the bench. "I should have come sooner. Much sooner."

Anna turned to look at him then, and Michael was struck by the evidence of sleepless nights in her eyes—a reflection of his own restless struggles over the past few days.

"I am glad you're here now," Anna observed.

"The last thing I wished to do was hurt you," Michael said gently, recalling that Samy had heard her crying. "Anna, I'm sorry. I never wanted to cause you pain."

"You didn't cause it," Anna replied, her voice stronger than he'd expected. "We both did, by assuming we knew what was best for each other without actually talking about it."

Michael felt a flutter of hope at her words. "You're right. I made assumptions about what you could handle, what you'd want, what would be fair to ask of you. I didn't trust you to make your own choices."

"And my reaction was to run away," Anna admitted. "I convinced myself that leaving was what was best for you. I know that running from someone important to me isn't the answer. I learned that lesson long ago when my parents did it to me."

"I'm sorry, Anna, for all you've been through. I know I can't really understand it, but I am so thankful you've chosen not to run away from what we have together."

"And I'm glad you understand enough not to judge me for it." Her soft hand gently squeezed his in a moment of sweet contact. "But God has truly worked all things out for my good."

"For *our* good." He whispered, as she leaned against his shoulder.

They sat in silence for a moment, both processing how their well-intentioned attempts to protect each other had nearly cost them everything.

"Anna," Michael said finally, "I need to ask you something, and I need you to answer honestly, without thinking about what you believe I want to hear."

Anna nodded, turning to face him fully.

"If there were a way—any possible way—for us to build a life together, would you want to try? Even if it meant significant changes for both of us?"

Anna's breath caught slightly, but her answer came without hesitation. "Yes. Michael, these past few days of avoiding each other have been miserable. Not just because I missed you, but because everything here feels incomplete without you in it."

Relief flooded through Michael's chest. "For me as well. The translation work, my daily routines, even my excitement about teaching—all of it felt hollow without you to share it with."

Michael reached for her hands, interlacing their fingers with the same sense of rightness he'd felt during the wedding celebration. "I want to make sure we're both clear about what we're choosing.

Anna, if we pursue this seriously, you would need to join our community. That means leaving your grandfather, your work at the museum, everything familiar in your life."

"I know," Anna replied steadily. "And you would be risking your teaching position, at least initially, and the disapproval of some community members who expected you to remain focused solely on your calling."

"Yes," Michael confirmed. "But my risks are minor compared to the sacrifices you would be making."

Anna was quiet for a long moment, her gaze returning to the horizon. When she spoke, her voice carried a certainty that surprised him.

"Michael, I've spent the past three days thinking about what my life in Ontario really offers me. It's safe, predictable, and comfortable. But it's also... limited. The work I do preserves the past, but it doesn't create anything new. I belong to a community, but I don't feel vital to it the way I've felt vital here."

"What do you mean?"

"I mean that in one week in New Hope, I've felt more useful, more connected, more alive than I have in years." Anna turned back to him, her eyes bright with conviction. "Yesterday, while helping Lydia, I found myself thinking about all the ways historical knowledge could be brought into daily life, how heritage could be made relevant to children, how stories could be preserved not just in museums but in living communities."

An excitement building in his chest energized him. "You're talking about creating something entirely new."

"Exactly. Michael, what if joining your community isn't about giving up my calling, but about finding a better way to fulfill it?"

The possibility sent warmth radiating through Michael's entire body. "You could teach in schools here, develop educational programs, help families preserve their own stories... even visit schools in Ontario when we'd go to visit your *dawdi*."

"Oh, I love the sound of that," Anna continued, her voice growing more animated. "There might be ways to combine what I love about my work with a life here that would be more fulfilling than anything I could build alone in Ontario."

Michael stared at her. "Anna, are you truly saying you want to join our community? Not as a sacrifice for love, but as a choice for your own faith and purpose?"

"I'm saying I want to build a life with you," Anna replied firmly. "And if that means joining your community, then I can't think of anything I'd rather do."

"What about your grandfather?"

Anna smiled, and Michael caught a glimpse of the woman who was brave enough to cross provinces to help him avoid matchmakers. "My grandfather has always encouraged me to listen for God's call in my life. When he suggested I accept your invitation, I think he hoped something like this might happen."

"Really?"

"He reminded me of his courtship with my grandmother," Anna said. "I'm thinking he was preparing me for exactly this choice."

The last of his reservations were dissolving. "And you're prepared for the complications it might cause? The fact that some people might disapprove, that it might take time for me to prove to the school board that I can balance courtship and marriage with teaching?"

"Are you prepared for those same complications?" Anna questioned him gently.

"With you beside me? I'm prepared for anything," Michael replied without hesitation.

Anna's smile was radiant.

Michael pulled her closer, marveling at how natural it felt to have her in his arms. "I love you," he said, the words feeling both familiar and miraculous.

"I love you too," Anna whispered back. "And Michael? I think we're going to be very fulfilled and happy together."

As they sat together in the growing morning light, Michael felt a deep sense of peace settle over him. There would still be challenges ahead with Joel and the school board, not to mention the emotional process of her leaving Ontario. But they would face those challenges together, as partners building something beautiful and new.

"There's one more thing," Anna said, pulling back to look at him with sparkling eyes. "I should probably warn you that Samy has been planning our wedding since about five minutes after we met."

Michael laughed, the sound carrying across the quiet farmyard. "In that case, we'd better court quickly. Samy doesn't like to be kept waiting."

"No," Anna agreed, settling back into his embrace. "And I don't want to wait long, either."

He couldn't agree more.

Anna walked hand-in-hand with Michael toward the Yoder farmhouse, her heart lighter than it had been in days. The decision they'd reached felt both monumental and perfectly natural—like stepping through a door she hadn't realized she'd been searching for her entire life.

"Are you nervous about telling your family?" Anna asked as they approached the house.

"About our decision?" Michael considered the question. "No. I think they'll be relieved more than anything. You?"

"Dawdi has been talking for some time about taking on our business manager full-time. Now I think about it, I believe this news will surprise him less than it has us." She considered how the Yoders would react, as she'd be telling them soon, too. "Samy has been so obviously frustrated with both of us for the past few days. I think she'll be delighted that we've finally come to our senses."

They paused at the bottom of the porch steps, both suddenly aware of the significance of the moment. Once they shared their decision, the process of building their life together would begin in earnest.

"Anna," Michael said quietly, "are you absolutely certain? I can give you time before we go tell everyone. Everything will be like a whirlwind once we do."

Anna studied his face, seeing the love and concern there, the genuine desire to protect her from making a choice she might regret. But she also saw something else—hope, excitement, the same sense of rightness that filled her own heart.

"Michael," she said firmly, "I've never been more certain of anything in my life."

His smile in response was brilliant with relief and joy. "In that case, shall we go change our lives?"

"Together," Anna agreed, squeezing his hand.

Before they reached the Yoders porch, Michael halted and drew her gently by her shoulders to face him. The love in his eyes stole her breath, as he tipped her chin up with his forefinger. She caught the hint of a smile on his lips as he leaned down to kiss her. Her eyes closed to enjoy the sweetness of the moment.

She had made the right choice. No doubt.

As they climbed the porch steps, Anna caught sight of Samy's face pressed against the kitchen window, her expression brightening as she spotted their joined hands. By the time they reached the door, the girl had disappeared, but Anna could hear excited whispers coming from inside the house.

"I think our news may not come as a complete surprise," Michael observed with amusement.

"I suspect she's been planning this outcome since the moment she accidentally sent your email."

The door opened before they could knock, revealing not just Samy but also Lydia and Joel, all three exuding barely contained curiosity and hope.

"Well?" Samy demanded without preamble. "Did you finally figure it out?"

Anna and Michael exchanged glances, then burst into laughter at the girl's characteristic directness.

"We figured it out," Michael confirmed, his arm tightening around Anna's waist.

"*Gott sei dank*," Lydia breathed, her face breaking into a wide smile. "The tension in this house for the past three days has been unbearable."

Joel's expression was more measured, but Anna could see approval and relief in his eyes. "I take it you've discussed the practical implications of your decision?"

"We have," Anna replied. "I'd like to speak with you about the process of joining your community, if you're willing to guide me through it."

"It would be my privilege," Joel said formally, though his tone carried warmth. "Though I should warn you, it's not a decision to be made lightly or quickly."

"I understand," Anna assured him. "I want to do this properly, to make sure I'm truly ready for the commitment I'm making."

"There's another matter to consider," Joel continued thoughtfully. "Your grandfather should be involved in this process."

Anna's face grew concerned. "I've been worrying about that. I don't want to exclude him, but—"

"Exclude him? Who said anything about leaving him out?" Joel interrupted with a small smile. "Anna, we want to invite him to visit, and I suspect he'll be on the first available transportation to Prince Edward Island."

"That will be fantastic." Michael's eyes brightened with hope. "My family will be delighted to have him stay for as long as he wants."

As they moved into the kitchen for what Anna suspected would be a long conversation about practical arrangements and plans, she felt a deep sense of gratitude for the unlikely matchmaker who had brought them to this moment. Samy's directness and wisdom had been exactly what they needed to overcome their own careful fears.

She tapped Samy on the shoulder and motioned her to a quiet corner of the room. "I just want to thank you, Samy. You've been a good friend. Honest and helpful and wanting what's best for me. And now, we can continue to be friends for a very long time."

Samy grew thoughtful. "That makes two new friends. All in one summer. Maybe I got the better deal."

Anna's gaze drifted to where Michael was busy talking to Joel. She didn't think so. Anna got the best deal, for sure. But she wouldn't tell Samy so, only look forward to the day when Samy discovered a lifetime love of her own.

And Anna would be in New Hope to see it all unfold alongside her new life. Indeed, she had found home.

Epilogue

Two months later - September, the first day of school

Samy stood outside her mother's shop in the crisp morning air, watching the familiar bustle of families preparing for the first day of the new school term. She clutched her slate and lunch pail, waiting for Sharon to meet her as they'd planned. This would be their first day as eighth graders under Michael's teaching, and despite her usual discomfort with change, Samy found herself genuinely excited.

Through the shop window, she could see Anna arranging a display of historical photographs and artifacts. The heritage corner had transformed her *mamm's* simple fabric store into something much more interesting—a place where people came not just to buy supplies but to learn about their community's history and preserve their family stories.

As Samy watched, Michael appeared in the doorway of the shop, his teacher's satchel over his shoulder and his face bright with the excitement of beginning his first official term. Anna looked up from her work, and the smile that spread across her face made Samy feel warm all over.

Michael crossed to Anna, said something that made her laugh, then leaned down to kiss her cheek in the gentle, respectful way that married couples in their community shared affection. Even from outside, Samy could see the happiness radiating from both of them.

"Have a *wunderbar* first day," Anna said, her voice carrying through the open door. "I'll have fresh cookies waiting when you come home."

"Save some for the students who don't give me too much trouble," Michael replied with a grin, glancing meaningfully toward the window where Samy stood.

Samy rolled her eyes but smiled. Michael had been teasing her about being his most challenging student ever since his engagement to Anna, though she could tell he was looking forward to having her in his classroom.

"Samy!" Sharon's voice called from down the path about ten minutes later. "Sorry I'm late. *Mamm* couldn't find my arithmetic book."

Sharon approached with her characteristic warm smile and her own school supplies neatly organized in a basket.

"Ready for our first day with Teacher Michael?" Sharon asked, falling into step beside Samy as they began walking toward the schoolhouse.

"*Ya*," Samy replied. "He might be more nervous than we are, though."

Sharon giggled. "It's sweet how worried he is about doing well. But my datt says anyone who can translate ancient journals and solve complicated romantic problems should be able to handle a one-room schoolhouse."

"Speaking of romantic problems," Samy said with satisfaction, and a bit of amazement that the subject of romance was more interesting to her than it had been before Anna came. Did that mean she was growing up? "You should have seen how happy they looked just now."

"I did," Sharon giggled. "It's amazing how everything worked out, isn't it? When you first told me about their pretend arrangement, I never imagined it would lead to this."

AMY GROCHOWSKI

Samy considered this as they walked. "I think it was always going to lead to this. They just needed help to get there."

"Help from a very wise fourteen-year-old," Sharon observed with a grin.

"Fifteen next month," Samy corrected. "And you helped too. Remember how you said they looked like they were really in love, even when they thought they were pretending?"

"I remember." Sharon sighed dreamily.

They walked in comfortable silence for a moment, both reflecting on the summer's dramatic events. Samy thought about how much had changed—not just for Michael and Anna, but for herself as well.

"Samy," Sharon said as the schoolhouse came into view, "I'm glad you decided to talk to me that first day at Noah's farm. Even if it was just about my rabbit."

"I'm glad you were patient with me," Samy replied honestly. "And that you didn't think I was too strange."

"Different isn't strange," Sharon said firmly. "It's just different. And sometimes different is exactly what people need."

As they approached the schoolhouse, they could see other students arriving with varying degrees of enthusiasm. The younger children bounced with excitement, while some of the older boys looked skeptical about having a new teacher.

"Do you think Michael will be strict?" Sharon asked, observing the gathering students.

"Fair but firm," Samy predicted. "He's not the type to let anyone get away with mischief, but he won't be mean about it either."

As they entered the schoolyard, she saw Michael in the doorway talking to Elijah Miller. She wondered what mischief Elijah had planned. He was a prankster. Samy felt a surge of protective affection for her future teacher and the man who had made Anna so happy. And she should warn Sharon too. He especially liked to tease pretty girls. And Sharon was very pretty.

"There's Myles," Sharon observed, nodding toward the Beller brothers who were approaching the school. "He looks pleased about something."

Samy followed her gaze to see Myles walking with his younger brothers, his expression relaxed and cheerful. At eighteen, he no longer attended school, but he often helped with outdoor maintenance projects.

"Probably happy that his brother gets to deal with Mason and Micah's energy instead of him," Samy said with amusement.

As the school bell rang and students began filing into the building, Samy and Sharon joined the stream of children. At the doorway, Michael greeted each student with a warm smile and an encouraging word.

"Hello again, Samy," he said when she reached him. "Ready for a year of learning?"

"Ready for a year of keeping you on your toes," Samy replied honestly, regretting it slightly when she heard Elijah laugh.

But Michael laughed too. "I wouldn't expect anything else. Good morning, Sharon. Welcome to our school."

"*Denki*," Sharon replied politely.

As they found their seats in the back of the classroom—the traditional place for eighth graders—Samy felt a rush of contentment sitting beside her new best friend.

"Class," Michael called from the front of the room, his voice carrying easily through the space, "welcome to a new school year. I'm honored to be your teacher, and I'm excited to learn alongside all of you."

Samy caught Sharon's eye and smiled. Whatever challenges this school year might bring, she was ready to face them with her best friend beside her and the knowledge that sometimes the most wonderful things came from the most unexpected beginnings.

After all, if an accidentally sent email could lead to a perfect match and marriage, what other good things might be waiting to be discovered?

As Michael began outlining the year's studies, Samy settled back in her seat with deep satisfaction. She had helped two people find their way to love, gained a dear friend, and learned to step outside her comfort zone.

Not a bad summer's work for someone who preferred horses to people. It seemed she was growing up, but not too fast, she hoped.

Amish Dreams on
PRINCE EDWARD ISLAND ~6~

An *Amish*
Heart's
Calling

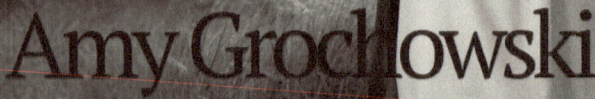

Amy Grochowski

ALSO BY AMY GROCHOWSKI

Amish Dreams on Prince Edward Island Series
An Amish Forever Home, #1
First Love at Christmas, #2
The Amish Runaway's Second Chance, #3
Home for an Amish Christmas, #4
A Match for the Amish Teacher, #5
An Amish Heart's Calling, #6
Amy's Love Inspired Amish Romance Books
The Amish Nanny's Promise
The Amish Baker's Secret Courtship
An Amish Love to Remember
A Secret Amish Arrangement

Learn More at www.amygrochowski.com